I was so nervous about starting secondary school.
Me — shy, ordinary Alice Grimes — going to Riverside
Academy for Girls! I thought it was for confident, clever,
posh people, not someone like me.

I was worried I wouldn't be able to do the work or get in
the teams and no one would want to be friends with me.

But most of all I was scared they'd find out my secret.
I had something to hide, you see. Something I didn't
want the girls of Riverside Academy to know about.

Have you got a secret? Something you feel you should
keep to yourself? If you have, I discovered it's much
better if you share it with someone. Someone you trust.

That's what friends are for.

Chris Higgins

The Secrets Club

Alice in the Spotlight

PUFFIN

PUFFIN BOOKS

Published by the Penguin Group
Penguin Books Ltd, 80 Strand, London WC2R ORL, England
Penguin Group (USA) Inc., 375 Hudson Street, New York, New York 10014, USA
Penguin Group (Canada), 90 Eglinton Avenue East, Suite 700, Toronto, Ontario, Canada M4P 2Y3
(a division of Pearson Penguin Canada Inc.)
Penguin Ireland, 25 St Stephen's Green, Dublin 2, Ireland (a division of Penguin Books Ltd)
Penguin Group (Australia), 250 Camberwell Road, Camberwell, Victoria 3124, Australia
(a division of Pearson Australia Group Pty Ltd)
Penguin Books India Pvt Ltd, 11 Community Centre, Panchsheel Park, New Delhi – 110 017, India
Penguin Group (NZ), 67 Apollo Drive, Rosedale, Auckland 0632, New Zealand
(a division of Pearson New Zealand Ltd)
Penguin Books (South Africa) (Pty) Ltd, Block D, Rosebank Office Park, 181 Jan Smuts Avenue,
Parktown North, Gauteng 2193, South Africa

Penguin Books Ltd, Registered Offices: 80 Strand, London WC2R ORL, England

puffinbooks.com

First published 2012
001 – 10 9 8 7 6 5 4 3 2 1

Text copyright © Chris Higgins, 2012
Illustrations copyright © Puffin Books, 2012
All rights reserved

The moral right of the author and illustrator has been asserted

Set in 13.5/17.5pt Baskerville by Palimpsest Book Production Limited,
Falkirk, Stirlingshire
Printed in Great Britain by Clays Ltd, St Ives plc

British Library Cataloguing in Publication Data
A CIP catalogue record for this book is available from the British Library

ISBN: 978-0-141-33522-3

www.greenpenguin.co.uk

MIX
Paper from
responsible sources
FSC™ C018179
www.fsc.org

Penguin Books is committed to a sustainable
future for our business, our readers and our planet.
This book is made from Forest Stewardship
Council™ certified paper.

ALWAYS LEARNING   **PEARSON**

For girls with secrets everywhere.

Great idea, Claire.

Thanks, Amanda.

Chapter 1

'Ready, Alice?' asks Mum, but she knows I am. I've been ready for weeks. Six actually. I've been ready since the first day of the summer holidays when she took me to town to buy my new school uniform.

Mum likes to be prepared. So do I.

Though if I'm being really honest, my things might be ready, but I'm not sure I am. Not deep inside.

I haul my new school bag up on to my shoulder. It's mega heavy. No wonder. It contains:

- an exercise book for every subject, all neatly covered and labelled
- a rough book
- a pocket-sized French dictionary
- a much bigger English dictionary with handy thesaurus

- files for IT and DT
- a geometry set
- a wallet containing emergency money
- a pencil case

All of them brand new and carefully chosen by me.

Inside the pencil case are new pencils, sharpened to within an inch of their lives; a new sharpener; new pens; a new rubber and new felt tips.

I love my new stuff. But I can't help feeling guilty about it. Particularly since I showed it to Austen and he pointed out that none of it had been recycled from primary school.

It was all Nikki's fault. She wanted to come with us that day to help me sort out my uniform and she insisted on treating me.

I did try. 'I don't need a new bag!' I'd protested. 'I've got a perfectly good one already. And a pencil case. And loads of biros and felt tips . . .'

I don't know why I bothered. She never listens to anyone.

'That tatty old stuff!' she'd jeered. 'New school, new beginning! Go mad for once, Ali. I'm paying.'

So I did.

My sister Nikki is always splashing her money around. Mum says now she's earning she should start putting some away for a rainy day, but Nikki doesn't do rainy days. She lives her life in permanent sunshine and it's money – not water – that pours through her fingers and down the drain.

I'm the opposite. I'm so careful. Nikki says it's painful. I can't help it. Mum says it's not that I'm mean, I'm a thinker, and she wishes Nikki would do a bit more thinking before jumping feet first into things.

I think about everything. Ever since Austen was put to sit next to me at the start of Year Four, I especially think about Consumerism and Waste and Global Warming and Saving the Planet. Austen was really into the environment and soon I was too. *The Eco-Twins*, our teacher called us.

Dad says it's like with Nikki every cloud has a silver lining, and with Alice every silver lining has a cloud. He used to want me to lighten up a bit, be more like her. But now he wants her to tone it down a bit. A lot. Especially after last night.

Nobody would ever think we were sisters. She's always laughing; I'm mostly serious. Though actually, we are kind of alike. Same dark hair, pale skin, wide brown eyes, high cheekbones and sort-of-pouty lips.

You can see the resemblance in her school photo when she was my age, though her eyes were all blotchy. Eleven years old and she was wearing make-up even then. She's unbelievable! She'd been made to wash her eyeliner and mascara off and her eyes were stinging from the soap, but she was still smiling for the camera.

But you'd have to look really close to see the likeness now. You see, I would never wear cosmetics because I read somewhere they're demeaning to women, plus Austen told me they're made from animal products. Anyway, I can't stand anything on my face. I even scrape my hair out of the way in a ponytail. Whereas Nikki's got to have hair extensions, false eyelashes, false nails and a full mask of make-up in place before she'd even consider going out of the front door.

'Come on, Trouble.' Dad's giving me a lift because it's my first day. He always calls me Trouble because I'm not. It's his sort of joke. He calls Nikki Angel, when they're speaking, that is, and she's definitely not angelic.

They're not speaking today; Nikki's staying well out of his way.

'Have a good time!' says Mum. She plants a kiss on my cheek and dashes upstairs to get ready for work.

Here we go. I pick up my PE kit in one hand and my lunch box in the other and wait in the narrow hallway while Dad gets the van out of the garage. My school bag bangs against the wall. I've got too much stuff. I want to take everything out and start all over again.

I've got stomach ache. I feel sick. I want to go back to bed.

I don't want to go to this new school any more.

Chapter 2

From behind me comes a giggle. 'Did you pack your bags yourself, madam?' Nikki intones, like she's in an airport. She's sitting on the top stair in her pyjamas, picking bits of polish off her nails.

'Yes, actually!' I say.

'Has he gone?'

'He's waiting outside.'

'Good. Got everything?'

'Yep,' I say, though I can't help doing a mental count again.

'Loosen your tie.'

'What for?'

'Cos you look like a nerd. You look like your boring mate Austen.'

I tug it down quickly. 'That's better,' she says. 'Now have fun.'

Fun. I stare at Nikki, fighting a sudden urge

to cry. What is fun about starting a new school where you know hardly anyone? It's all her fault I'm going to Riverside Academy for Girls on my own. All my friends, including Austen, are going to the local mixed comprehensive down the road where Nikki went, but Mum and Dad didn't think it was 'appropriate' for me.

'You mean, you want to keep her away from the boys in case she turns out like me,' Nikki had said mockingly, and Mum said, 'No, but Alice is a bright girl. She should have a stab at the entrance test.'

'You didn't put *me* in for it. Does that mean I'm not bright?' said Nikki with a glint in her eye, and Mum said, 'Of course you're bright!' and then Dad joined in and said, 'You could've gone to university if you'd tried,' and Nikki said, 'I didn't want to go to flaming university!' and then they had another big row.

No one asked me what I wanted to do.

In the end, I agreed to sit the entrance test for Riverside for two reasons:

1. To keep Mum and Dad happy.
2. Because, if by some amazing fluke I did get in, at least I wouldn't be in Nikki's shadow any more.

I knew I'd fail it anyway. Everyone, including Mum, thinks I'm dead clever because I'm a 'thinker', but I'm not. I have to work hard to keep up.

But, to my huge surprise, I passed. And that was it.

'You're going to Riverside!' said Mum, over the moon with excitement. 'No argument! It's a great school.'

It is. I know it is. I've been there. I sat my test in the Great Hall along with hundreds of other candidates. It was like something out of *Harry Potter*. It was old and smelt of polish and I liked it. It had wooden floors and high ceilings and on the walls were shields and boards with lists of names on them and pictures of past headmistresses. A bit of me is excited about going there, but most of me wishes I was just going down the road with my friends from primary school. With Austen.

'Hey?' Nikki's voice is soft. 'You'll be fine, Worry-guts.'

I raise my eyes to hers. 'You reckon?' It's all right for her to say that – my cool, popular, don't-give-a-damn sister.

Her face is scrubbed clean. Even in the state she came home in last night, she still wouldn't go to bed without doing her beauty routine. She looks younger without make-up. She looks her age. Nineteen.

'You don't want to go to my school,' she says, reading my mind. 'It was a dump.'

'You did all right,' I concede, for the first time ever.

'Yeah, I did, didn't I?' she says, looking surprised and pleased at the same time. Then her face falls. 'Tell that to Mum and Dad.'

'They're proud of you,' I say, though we both know this is not entirely true.

Nikki snorts. 'Not this morning, they're not.' Then she says, 'Better get a move on. You don't want to be late on your first day.'

She comes downstairs and gives me a hug. My sister smells of perfume, alcohol and bed.

'I won't know anyone there, Nik,' I whisper. Her arms tighten round me.

'You will soon! You'll make loads of new mates. Everybody loves Alice!'

'No, they don't!' I say automatically, but it cheers me up to hear her say it. 'What if I can't do the work?'

'You can! You're a right brain-box!'

'I wish!' But what I really wish is that I was as brave as Nikki. Nothing scares her.

Dad sounds his horn outside.

'Go on, Misery-guts is waiting,' says Nikki.

'I don't want to!' I say and I mean it. But then Mum comes out of the bathroom and stares at me in surprise.

'Are you still here? Nikki, what are you up to? You're making her late!'

'My fault, as usual!' says my sister, even though it isn't. She pushes me gently away. 'Go on, sprat! You can do this!'

Dad sounds the horn again and yells, 'Alice!' and Nikki yells back, 'Keep your hair on!' and then *she* gets it in the neck, not me, because Dad is still cross with her.

Last night my sister was brought home in a police car. She was brawling in the street and they said if she did it again they'd arrest her for causing a public disturbance and she'd spend a night in the cells. My parents were mortified, and so was I. Some of the stuff she gets up to makes me want to curl up and die.

Just thinking about last night again is making me cringe. I decide then and there that nobody – and I mean NOBODY – is going to find out about my sister at my new school.

Chapter 3

When we pull into Riverside Road behind billions of cars dropping off trillions of girls, my mouth goes dry. Some of them look so old. As old as Nikki! I can't help noticing how stylish they all look, even in school uniform, as they pour through the gates. How do they do that? I'll have to ask Nikki; she knows about these things. I can see now it's only the little ones, the new ones like me, who've got their ties done up tight. I loosen mine some more. I don't want to look like a nerd.

It's no good; I feel a fraud in my blazer with the school crest on it. It's too big for me. I'm like a little kid tottering around in her mum's high heels, pretending to be grown-up.

Dad tries to park outside the front gates, but he can't pull in and the car behind him honks impatiently when he slows down. I turn round.

It's a woman in a flashy little sports car. Nikki would love that. Dad mutters under his breath and keeps going.

At the end of the road he turns left and I think, *Just carry on driving, Dad, anywhere, I don't mind where, so long as it's as far away as possible from this strange new school with its high walls and long, narrow windows.* I feel like crying, again. I never cry!

My old school was modern, warm and welcoming; this new one looks like a Victorian prison.

In my old school I knew everyone; in this new one, I won't know a soul.

But he turns left and left again and, before we know it, we're back in Riverside Road and this time Dad sees a gap to pull into. He drives past and stops, flicking on his indicator to show he's about to reverse into the space, but the sports car, which must have followed us round, nips into it before he can. He swears loudly and profusely, but the woman doesn't even look at us; she's too busy helping her daughter and her piles of bags out of the car.

She looks posh. You can tell because she's wearing slacks and one of those gilet things and she's got a string of pearls round her neck. Dad winds down the window and my heart sinks.

'Oi!' he says. 'You!' The woman looks up in surprise. 'That was my space!'

'Really?' The woman raises her eyebrows. 'I didn't realize it had your name on it.'

'I was reversing into it.'

'Sorry! I thought you'd gone past it. Look, I'm in a bit of a rush . . .'

'We're all in a flaming rush!' says my dad, warming up.

'Dad! Leave it!' I mutter. He's acting like Nikki.

The woman ignores him completely. 'Come on, Melissa. I want a word with the headteacher before school . . .'

'Mu-um! I can go in on my own. I'm not helpless!' The girl standing by the car certainly doesn't look helpless. She's tall and slim with long fair hair trailing down her back, held by clips that are super-expensive. I know, because Nikki's got them.

'I need to explain to her all about your . . .' The woman turns away and I miss the rest of the sentence as she marches purposefully towards the gates with an armful of bags. The girl scowls and trails after her.

'Bloody cheek!' snarls Dad through the open

window as a parting shot. Another car starts hooting behind him and he knocks the van into gear and we jerk forward and stall. The car behind blasts its horn and my dad swears loudly again.

The posh woman turns round and glares at him. 'Really!' she says in disgust. Then she barks at the girl as if she doesn't want her anywhere near us, 'Come on, Melissa!'

I am soooo embarrassed I don't know where to look. It's not like my dad to swear at someone in the street. I'm not making excuses for him because he was way out of order, but I think he was still upset about Nikki and last night. But now he's being just as bad as her. Worse!

I am *never* going to live this down! I haven't even set foot in school yet and that girl must hate me already. When word gets round, everyone will hate me!

He restarts the van and I shriek, 'Stop! I'll get out here!' and he jerks to a halt. The car behind us honks furiously again and my dad sticks his head out of the window and bellows obscenities at the driver. By now, everyone is staring at us, shocked.

Cheeks on fire, I jump out and open the back

of the van to get my stuff. I refuse to look up, but I can hear the gasps and tuts of disapproval and giggles, and even the odd, muted cheer. Then someone gets out of the car behind us and marches past me, sweeping me to one side, and everyone falls silent. It's a tall woman with iron-grey hair and a very straight back, and she stops at Dad's window.

'How dare you speak to me like that!' she says and, though her voice is quiet and controlled, her eyes are like flint and I go cold with fear.

'I'll speak to you how I like!' sneers Dad. 'Who do you think you are?'

'The headmistress,' she says. 'And who, may I ask, are you?'

I want to die.

Chapter 4

It was an angel who rescued me. An angel with a smiling face and big brown eyes and hair plaited into hundreds of tiny braids, each one with a shiny blue or yellow bead at the end: school colours.

I stand there listening to my dad spluttering apologies at the head and I want to run away. I really do. But then I feel an arm slipping through mine and a voice as warm and comforting as hot chocolate says, 'Come on, we don't want to be late. Shall I take this?'

The girl has picked up my bag. She tugs me gently and I move away from my dad's grovelling voice and follow her obediently through the school gates. I feel like I'm blind and she's my faithful guide-dog because somehow she must have negotiated me through the milling crowds and up the steps and through the front doors.

I end up sitting next to her in the Great Hall, among rows and rows of people in brand-new uniform, flanked by two aisles of teachers, and I haven't a clue how I got there. The ceiling is high and vaulted, and, from the walls, portraits of past headmistresses glare down at me. I sit on my hands and sink further into my seat, trying to avoid their disapproving eyes.

The girl turns to me and smiles. 'It's horrible being new, isn't it?' she whispers and I nod, too scared to speak.

At the end of the hall is a stage.

And walking on to the stage is the headmistress.

We all get to our feet.

The head's name is Mrs Shepherd. She introduces herself and welcomes us all to our new school, then we sing the hymn 'The Lord is My Shepherd', which is kind of appropriate, I guess. Then she tells us all to sit down and makes a long speech about *New Opportunities* and *Seizing the Day* and how *The World is Our Oyster but It's up to Us to Turn the Grit to Pearls*. I like the idea of this, though I'm worried that she's got me down already as too gritty to ever make a decent pearl, the kind that woman who pinched our parking space would wear. The girl beside me rolls her eyes and, even though I'm nervous, I have to suppress a giggle. She reminds me of Nikki.

'Here at Riverside Academy, we want you all to be fully involved in school life,' continues Mrs Shepherd and she tells us about their *Gold Standard* hockey, netball, tennis and athletics teams, and the girl next to me sits up and takes notice. I bet she's *Gold Standard* at sport. I'm not. I'm more *Rusty Metal*. But then the head outlines various other clubs and activities we can take part in, including the School Council which is made up of teachers and pupils who help run the school, and I think that sounds really interesting.

When the speech is over, Mrs Shepherd reads out a list of who's going into which class. I'm scared that my name won't be on there, that it's all a mistake, I shouldn't be here. Then I'm scared that if it is she'll glare at me, so I sit there, holding my breath. But when she finally reads my name out she just carries on to the next one as if she didn't even notice. At the end we wait to be called out by our form teachers.

'Which class are you in?' says my saviour, her face alight with excitement.

'I'm in 7LW.'

Her face lights up even more. 'Me too!' she says. 'Shall we sit together?'

'All right then,' I say, as coolly as I can, but I can't help myself grinning from ear to ear. 'What's your name?'

'Tasheika,' she says. 'Tasheika Campbell. What's yours?'

'Alice. Alice Grimes.'

'Cool.' She grins at me like it's the best name in the world. 'That's our form teacher over there.' She points to a slim young woman with shoulder-length dark hair, wearing straight-cut trousers and a lacy cardigan. She's got a badge on that says *Miss Webb*, and she looks nice.

'Her name's Linda Webb,' explains Tasheika. 'That's why we're called 7LW. She's going to take us for English too.'

'How do you know?' I ask curiously.

She shrugs and her braids bounce around her face. I wonder if I could do my hair like that. 'I just do,' she says. 'I must've read it somewhere.'

I stare at her in admiration. She already knows her way around.

'Come on,' she says. 'We're lining up.'

I follow my new friend into line. Miss Webb smiles at me and I smile back.

Maybe I'm going to like it here after all.

Chapter 5

Miss Webb leads us through a maze of corridors to our new classroom, pointing out things as we go past. I sneak a look through doors and windows and see rows of girls with their hands in the air or writing furiously with bent heads, their teachers standing at the front. I hear faint snatches of conversations as we pass, half a question here, the tail of an answer there, or the short, sharp bark of a command.

'It's so quiet!' whispers Tasheika, her brown eyes wide with surprise. 'Not a bit like my last school.'

'Nor mine!' I say with a pang, remembering the constant buzz of conversation in my Year Six classroom where I sat at nice round tables with my friends, Austen always by my side.

'And this is the dining hall where you eat your lunch,' points out Miss Webb with a flourish.

'The dining hall!' giggles Tasheika. 'It sounds so posh! We called it the canteen in my last school!'

'So did we!'

'Library on your right, or should I say, the Learning Resources Centre . . . down here is the Sports Hall . . . opposite, Computer Room A. Computer Room B is upstairs. Toilets here on the left . . .' Miss Webb sweeps us along.

'I'm never going to remember where everything is!' I say in alarm.

'Nor me!' says Tasheika, but I know she will and resolve to stick close to her.

We come to a halt outside a classroom and Miss Webb tells us that she is going to read out our names again and we must make sure we line up in alphabetical order. Tasheika is near the front of the queue, but I have to wait a bit before my name is called. And then the teacher says, 'Melissa Hamilton,' and the tall girl with the long fair hair and the nice clips, and the posh mother my dad swore at, detaches herself from the ones who are left and comes to stand behind me. I freeze, praying she won't recognize me.

Then Miss Webb says, 'Right then, we will

move into the classroom and you will sit in alphabetical order. Fill up the seats from the front please. No gaps.'

My heart sinks. I'm not going to be next to nice, friendly Tasheika after all. I'm going to have to sit by someone who looks as if she had a dining hall not a canteen in her last school and, once I turn round and she sees who I am, is going to hate me.

Unless I get paired with the girl in front . . . But when I look at the girl in front of me she and the girl in front of *her* are grabbing each other's hands and saying, 'Yes! We get to sit together!' and it's obvious they're best friends from primary school. They even look alike with the same identical haircuts and studs in their ears.

I decide I wouldn't want to sit by a clone who wants to hold hands with me anyway. Which leaves me with Posh Girl. I stand there, consumed with despair.

Then someone says, 'Excuse me, Miss Webb. May I go to the toilet?'

How embarrassing is that?

'Can't you wait?' Miss Webb sounds cross.

'No, sorry, Miss.' It's Tasheika. She doesn't sound embarrassed.

'Hurry up then. The rest of you, inside.'

As Tasheika passes, she winks at me. 'Keep me a seat,' she whispers and I feel myself smiling.

We all file into the classroom. It's set out in rows of tables, each sitting two people. We fill up from the front, as instructed. The two clones sit safely down together. I sit behind them, last but one from the back, plonking my bag on the seat next to me.

'Excuse me,' says the girl with long hair. 'I think that's my seat.' Her voice is clear and confident, like she's used to getting her own way.

'I'm really sorry,' I say. 'I'm keeping it for someone.'

Her eyebrows rise. 'You're not allowed to do that.'

'I know.' My voice comes out in a whisper. I don't know what to do. The last thing I want is to get into an argument like my dad – like Nikki.

'You can sit by me if you like,' says a voice behind us. We both turn round and stare at the owner of the voice in surprise. A boy with sandy hair and freckles has sat himself at the table behind us. 'My name's Danny and I don't bite.'

'I didn't know boys were allowed in this school,' says Melissa.

'They're not. Unfortunately. I'm Dani with an *i*.

24

Danielle, actually.' He grins at us and now I can see he is a she, even though her hair's cropped short like a boy's.

Melissa goes pink. 'Sorry,' she mutters.

'That's all right,' says Dani cheerfully. 'I don't mind.'

'We are waiting for you to sit down, Melissa,' says Miss Webb and, covered in confusion, Melissa sinks into the seat next to Dani without another word.

'Miss, where's my seat?' Tasheika is back in the classroom, glancing innocently around.

'Oh dear, we forgot to keep a seat for you,' says the teacher, sounding a bit cross. 'Now we'll all have to move up one.'

'Please, Miss, there's a spare one here,' I say, putting my hand up.

'There shouldn't be.' Miss Webb frowns. 'Melissa, you should have sat next to Alice. It's not up to you to decide who you sit by. I told you not to leave any gaps.'

My blood runs cold as the girl gasps at the injustice of it all. She opens her mouth to object. 'But . . .'

'Oh, never mind,' says our form teacher impatiently. 'Tasheika, go and sit by Alice.'

'Yes, Miss,' says Tasheika, as meek as a kitten, and she walks down the aisle towards me, her eyes sparkling. *Result!* she mouths at me, with her back to Miss Webb. As she takes her seat beside me, I hear a growl of annoyance from the table behind and I can't help turning round. Melissa is glaring at me.

But, beside her, Dani is grinning from ear to ear.

'Turn round, Alice!' says Miss Webb and I do so quickly. I don't want to get into any more trouble on my first day.

I've already made an enemy and it's not even breaktime.

Chapter 6

Before I came to Riverside Academy, there were loads of things I was nervous about. I'd made a *Things to be Concerned About at My New School* list.

1. Will anyone speak to me?
2. Will I be able to find my way around?
3. Will everyone be really posh?
4. Will I make friends?
5. Will I be able to do the work?
6. Will I get bullied?
7. Will I make the teams?
8. Will anyone find out that Nikki is my sister?

Nikki had found it and laughed and went, 'Yes, yes, yes, yes, yes, yes and yes,' which was kind of comforting on the whole, except for questions three and six. But then she came to question eight and she looked hurt and said, 'Are you ashamed of me?'

I'd felt really bad then. 'Of course not, it was a joke!' I'd said and crossed it off. But it wasn't.

I should have added another one instead.

8. Will I make any enemies?

When the bell goes for break, Miss Webb reminds us where the toilets and the dining hall are.

Tasheika turns to me, her face bright with excitement. 'Do you need the loo?'

'No!' What a weird question to ask. My surprise must have shown in my face because she laughs.

'Sorry! I'm used to looking after my little brothers! Come on then! Let's go outside and explore.'

'Wait for me!' says Dani. 'Coming?' she asks Melissa and my heart sinks but she doesn't reply. 'Suit yourself!' adds Dani cheerfully and follows Tasheika and me outside into the sunshine.

'Let's sit here,' she says and we park ourselves on a high, grassy bank overlooking the school field.

To my surprise, I see that Melissa has decided to join us after all. She sits down next to us as

Tasheika announces, 'I'm Tasheika, but you can call me Tash.'

'But Tasheika's so pretty!' I protest. 'Why would you want to shorten it?'

'It's such a mouthful.'

'My mother hates names being shortened,' remarks Melissa in her loud, clear voice, and I find myself cringing with shame at the mention of her mother. She already hates me for getting her into trouble with Miss Webb. I wonder if she's worked out yet it was my dad who yelled at her mum?

Dani snorts. 'Well, my name is Danielle, but don't you ever dare call me that. I like to be known as Dani.'

'Suits you,' says Melissa.

'Yeah. Everyone thinks I'm a boy.'

'No, they don't,' says Tash kindly.

'Yes, they do! *She* did!'

So did I, but I keep quiet.

'I'm sorry,' says Melissa and goes pink again. Dani laughs.

'It's OK, I don't mind. I wish I *were* a boy.'

'Why?'

'Then I could play football.'

'Girls can play football,' Tash points out.

'Not here, they can't!' groans Dani. 'How did I end up in an all-girls' school?' She looks so mournful that we all laugh, and then she laughs too.

'I want to play hockey,' says Melissa.

'Me too!' chorus the other two.

'And netball,' says Tash and everyone agrees, so I do too. But the truth is I'm useless at games and I bet they'll all be brilliant.

I can feel Melissa staring at me, unsmiling. 'What did you say your name was?'

I swallow hard. 'Alice.'

'Can we call you Ali?' asks Dani. She nods at Melissa. 'I don't care what her mum says, I like shortening my friends' names. It shows you like them.'

Dani's words give me a warm glow inside. 'If you want,' I say.

'Good.' She turns to Melissa. 'What are you called, then?'

'Melissa.'

'That's a mouthful too. I'm going to call you Mel.'

Melissa looks startled.

'Unless you don't want me to because your mum won't like it,' concedes Dani.

'No, it's not that. I'm just not sure *I* like it.'

'How about Lissa then?' asks Tash. 'That's nice.'

'Lissa.' She tries it out on her tongue, like a new taste she's got to get used to. 'No one's ever called me that before.'

'Really?' Dani stares at her in surprise. 'Well, you're Lissa now.'

And the newly christened Lissa looks quite pleased about it.

'Lissa, Dani, Ali and Tash. Sounds good,' says Tash with satisfaction, and we all agree. I take a deep breath and turn to Lissa.

'I'm really sorry about getting you into trouble with Miss Webb. About the seat.'

'Ah, that was all my fault, babe!' announces Tash breezily, like it's no big deal. 'I told Ali to keep it for me.' Then she turns to Dani and starts talking about football.

Lissa shrugs. 'It's all right,' she says to me. 'I think I'm going to like sitting next to Dani.'

So far, so good. I take another deep breath. 'And, um, sorry about the mix-up earlier as well.'

'What mix-up?'

'About the parking space.'

She stares open-mouthed at me. 'Was that you?

I mean, was that your dad? The one who swore at my mum?'

'He doesn't do that normally. He was just in a bad mood this morning,' I say in a rush. 'I'm really, really sorry.'

Her eyes are wide with disbelief. 'No one ever speaks to her like that,' she says.

I want to sink through the ground. This is where it all goes wrong. I knew I was never going to fit in here. 'He swore at the head too,' I say miserably. 'It wasn't personal.'

'Wow!' She contemplates this for a while then, to my surprise, says feelingly, 'Parents, hey? Super-embarrassing!'

I smile at her, weak with relief, and she smiles back. She may come from a posh family but somehow I get the impression she finds them just as annoying as I find mine.

The bell sounds for the end of break and we scramble to our feet.

'Where are we going next?' asks Dani.

'Science,' answers Tash. 'Those are the science labs over there.'

'Come on!' shouts Lissa and we chase after her obediently.

Mentally I run through the numbers on my

Things to be Concerned About list as we file into science and Tash squeezes in next to me. After break, Day One, and already I can tick off the first four.

1. Yes, people have spoken to me.
2. Yes, I'm beginning to find my way around.
3. No, not everyone is posh and even if they are (like Lissa), they can still be nice.
4. And, yes, I'm starting to make friends already! (Fingers crossed!)

Riverside Academy is turning out to be way more fun than I thought it would be.

Chapter 7

That night I ring Austen to find out how his first day at school went. Austen Penberthy is my best friend from primary school. My best friend, NOT my boyfriend. He is tall and thin with fair curly hair, glasses and a nice face, and he's an eco-warrior.

I think that's why we're best mates, because we've got lots in common. We're a bit more serious-minded than most people. Like I said, it's Austen who got me interested in the environment in the first place. His family is into saving the planet, unlike mine. They grow their own food and keep chickens and recycle everything. Dad calls him Earthy Penberthy.

'What you doing?' I ask.

'Collecting worms for the compost heap.'

'How did it go?'

'Good. There are loads around because it's been raining.'

'I meant school. What was it like?'

'All right. Did you know that earthworms have to come to the surface when it rains or they drown?'

'No, I didn't. Did you make any friends?'

'Um, one or two.' I feel a slight pang. *I'm Austen's friend.* But then he says, 'The trouble is they'll die if they're exposed to direct sunlight.'

'Really?' I laugh out loud. 'What are they? Vampires?'

'What?'

Immediately I feel bad. 'Oh no, I'm sorry! Poor things! Have they got that condition where your hair is white and your eyes are pink? What's it called?'

'Albinism? It's lack of pigmentation.' He pauses. 'What are you talking about?'

'Your new friends – who can't go out in the sun because they'll die.'

There's silence. Then he says, 'I was talking about earthworms.'

I should've known. It's hard to sidetrack Austen from a subject he's interested in. I wait for him to ask me about my day, but he launches into how important earthworms are in the food chain because not only do they enrich and aerate the soil but birds eat them as well.

Normally I would find this interesting, but I want him to stop so I can tell him about Tash and Dani and Lissa. But I can't get a word in edgeways and in the end I have to go because I need to get on with my homework.

Today I have made a discovery. Girls are better at listening than boys.

I can't wait to get to school tomorrow and see my new friends again.

'Your dad will drop you off on his way to work,' says Mum the next day at breakfast.

'No way!'

Mum looks at me in surprise. 'Don't be like that, Alice! It's very kind of your father to take you to school.'

'I can find my own way, thank you,' I say frostily, and Mum and Nikki stare first at me, then at Dad who is avidly studying the box of cornflakes, and then at each other.

'What's going on?' asks Mum suspiciously.

Dad tears his eyes away from the cornflakes and looks at his watch. 'Gosh, is that the time?'

he says, leaping to his feet. 'Best be off!'

'Colin?' Mum follows him out to the hall, but she's too late; the front door slams behind him. She comes back in clutching the newspaper. 'What was all that about?' she says.

I shrug, my mouth full of toast. I'm not going to split on Dad even if he was seriously out of order yesterday. Mum would go bananas if she knew what he'd done. But there was no way I was going to repeat the performance and risk him upsetting someone else.

Anyway, I've arranged to meet Tash at the bus stop midway between our houses this morning. We don't live that close, either side of the bypass, but she said she'd cross the bridge and meet me on my side so we could catch the bus to school together.

I get there early, but there's no sign of her so I let one bus go. It starts to rain. I keep checking my watch – still no Tash. Ten minutes later the next one pulls in, and I don't know what to do. If I don't get this one the next one could be another ten minutes – it'll be nearly registration . . . What a dilemma! I don't want to go without her, but I'm getting soaked and I can't be late on my second day.

Will she hate me if I go without her?

I can see the driver getting ready to pull out and I'm leaping from one foot to the other in an agony of indecision when I see her charging towards me, beads flying. We jump on to the bus and she flashes her pass at the driver and slumps into a seat, breathless, while I pay for my ticket.

'How come you've got a pass?' I ask as I take my seat beside her.

'I get free travel.' She grins at me in relief. 'I thought I was going to miss the bus.'

'Why were you late?'

'I had to take Keneil to nursery.'

'Who's Keneil?'

'My little brother.'

I wonder why her mum didn't take him and I'm just about to ask when Tash says, 'Did you get your English homework done?'

'Yeah.'

'Me too. Look!' She pulls her English book out of her bag and shows me pages and pages of nice neat writing entitled *All About Me*.

'You've done loads!' I say admiringly.

'Yeah. I like English; it's my favourite subject, next to PE. I love reading and writing.'

That's pretty obvious. But she's such an

interesting person she'd have had loads to write about anyway. 'Mine's not very long,' I say doubtfully.

'It's quality, not quantity that counts,' says Tash kindly, but that doesn't reassure me. I'm OK at factual things, like geography and science; I love reading all about our planet and how it works. That's why everyone thinks I'm brainy. But creative stuff I'm not so good at. It took me ages last night to get my homework done; I couldn't get going at all. There's not really much to say about me. Compared to Tash, I'm pretty boring.

In the end Mum told me to stop worrying about it and just write about what I liked best. So I made notes on my favourite topic and read them back to Mum and Dad. Dad didn't listen because he was watching the football, but Mum said it was brilliant.

But she's my mum – she doesn't count.

I don't know if anyone else will find it interesting.

Chapter 8

In English Miss Webb asks us if anyone would like to come out the front and read her *All About Me* to the class and a forest of hands shoots up. Not mine.

'We'll go round the class,' says Miss Webb, 'then everyone will get a chance. We'll start with . . . you.' And she points at Lissa whose arm stretches up highest.

Lissa reads hers out in a loud voice that makes us all pay attention. She tells us how she lives with her mum and dad and her older brother in a big house and she likes skiing and horse riding. Her brother is captain of the rugby team at his school. She learnt to play the violin by the Suzuki method and her mum learnt it with her and she has piano lessons too, but really she'd like to drop them and concentrate on sport, but her mum won't let her. Her dad works in finance and her mum is a homemaker and is on lots of committees.

'What do you want to do when you leave school, Melissa?' asks Miss Webb.

'Travel, go to university, then do something interesting in the city. In that order,' says Lissa without hesitating.

Miss Webb nods her head as if this is what she expected Lissa to say.

We all clap politely.

Dani goes next. Hers isn't very long which makes me feel better.

She says she lives with her mum and younger sister because her mum and dad are divorced. She says she used to go to football matches with her dad when she was little, but now he's married again and moved away and he's got two stepsons and takes them instead. She says she wishes she'd been born a boy because they have more fun. Everyone laughs but for some reason this makes me feel a bit sad.

She ends by saying, 'When I grow up I want to be a professional footballer,' and we all laugh again, because we didn't expect that. And also it's funny to hear Dani say, 'When I grow up,' because she's so short and looks quite young. Dani doesn't mind; she just grins at us all.

Miss Webb doesn't laugh though. She says, very seriously, 'Dani, you can be anything you want in life if you put your mind to it.' And Dani's grin stretches so much her eyes practically disappear as everyone gives her a clap.

I like Miss Webb.

We keep going round the class and I get to find out more about my classmates. Some girls sound really posh, like Lissa, and some sound really grown-up, like a girl called Georgia, and some sound really clever, like Nisha, but soon they all start to sound the same. The two clones who sit in front of us are called Chloe and Emma and their *All About Me*s are practically identical, which isn't surprising because so are they.

It gets a bit boring to be honest. After a while I stop listening.

But then it's Tash's turn.

She dances out to the front and starts reading, but it feels more like she's talking to us, or even singing. She's got a lovely voice, warm and soft, but lively at the same time, like your favourite music, and everyone sits up and listens.

'My mum is called Comfort,' she begins and
Dani says, 'What a great name for a mum!' and
everyone laughs, including Tash. She carries on,
saying, 'And my brothers are called Marlon,
Devon and Keneil. Marlon is ten and he's
football-mad, Devon is eight and likes break-
dancing and Keneil is three and he's into
dinosaurs and space-rockets and transformers.'

'Aahh!' says everyone and Tash's eyes shine,
and her beads bob around her head as she carries
on describing them so well you feel like they're
right there in front of you. Her stories about
what they get up to make us laugh and make me
wish I had little brothers too. You can tell she
loves them to bits.

'What about your dad?' asks Dani when Tash
finally comes to a halt. 'You haven't mentioned
him.'

Just for a second, Tash looks sad. 'He's not
around any more.' And Dani nods because she
knows what that feels like.

'Tell us more about your mum then,' says Miss
Webb gently. Tash's face lights up again.

'My mum is awesome! She looks after us all
. . . and she's got a great job . . . and she's a
brilliant cook! She makes fabulous cakes, not just

for birthdays but like every day . . . and she's really creative . . . she can sew and knit and do all that stuff . . . and –'

'Whoa! We'd better stop you there. You're very lucky to have such a lovely mum, Tasheika,' interrupts Miss Webb and Tash says, 'Yes, I am, Miss,' and everyone claps.

'Now what would you like to be when you leave school?' asks our form teacher.

'That's easy,' says Tash. 'I would like to be Alana de Silva.'

A big cheer goes up. Alana de Silva is a local girl made good – or bad – depending on your point of view. She's a model-cum-singer-cum-TV-presenter-cum-media-celebrity and is constantly in the newspapers and magazines, or on television or YouTube. Two years ago, no one had heard of her; now she's everywhere.

Miss Webb rolls her eyes and laughs.

'It sounds like everyone else does too!' she says. But then some people, Dani included, start shouting out things like, 'I don't!' and 'She's rubbish!' and stuff like that.

When Lissa says, 'She's a chav,' in a really snobby voice, Tash bristles and says, 'No, she's not, she's amazing!' And then it seems that

44

everyone has an opinion on Alana de Silva that they want to voice VERY LOUDLY INDEED, except for me, and Miss Webb shouts, 'That's enough!' and everyone quietens down.

'Now then, it's Alice's turn,' she says. 'Do you want to be Alana de Silva, Alice?'

I take a deep breath. 'No, I don't,' I say. 'I want to save the planet.'

Chapter 9

I tell everyone that I live with my mum and dad and my older sister and I want to protect the world we live in. Tash smiles at me encouragingly. She knows how nervous I am. I begin reading.

'I am really interested in the environment. Global warming is a problem that affects us all.' I look up and see Lissa nodding in agreement and take heart. 'We need to save the rain forests, eliminate the problem of toxic waste, be aware of the perils of acid rain, consider alternative sources of energy to fossil fuels and protect the world's precious species.'

Soon I get into my stride and before long I can't stop. It's known as the Austen Effect! By the time I've dealt with these topics I'm really warmed up and am about to launch into a favourite subject of mine, water pollution, when Miss Webb butts in.

'Well, you've certainly given us something to think about,' she says. 'Everyone's been listening most attentively. Has anyone got any questions they'd like to ask Alice?'

At first I'm pleased with the effect my talk has had on everyone. Instead of the outburst at the end of Tash's, there's a sort of stunned silence, like everyone's pretty impressed. Most people have got a glazed expression on their face, like they're deep in thought about what I've told them. But then I notice one or two girls have got their eyes closed and it dawns on me that instead of making them think, maybe I've bored them to death. I wait desperately for someone to ask a question. At last, Dani takes pity on me.

'I don't get global warming. Why is it so bad if the weather gets warmer?'

'Yeah, I like it when the sun shines!' says Georgia.

I'm not too sure about Georgia. She seems way older than me and she's *very* confident.

'It rains too much in this country,' says her friend, whose name I don't know yet, but who seems way older than me too.

'Well, it's not quite as simple as that,' I say and give them an in-depth description of carbon dioxide and methane as greenhouse gases. I explain about fossil fuels at some length in order to lead up to the problem of the melting ice caps and the terrible effect this has on poor polar bears, which is a very sad topic. But to my dismay I notice that people are yawning and looking at their watches.

'Thank you for a very informative talk, Alice,' says Miss Webb. 'Now sit down please.'

'I haven't finished yet!' I say. Then I see Georgia rolling her eyes at her friend and her friend smirking so I sit down quickly.

'There's always lunchtime!' says my teacher.

But at lunchtime the only thing that people want to talk about is Alana de Silva.

Alana de Silva is the girl everyone wants to be.

Unless you're a tomboy like Dani, or posh like Melissa, or a thinker like me. Or a few others in my new class who appear to dislike her intensely.

It's probably truer to say that Alana de Silva is a girl you either love or hate. It seems that no one feels neutral about her.

'My mother can't bear her,' says Lissa, which doesn't surprise me a bit.

'Nor mine!'

'Nor mine!'

Everyone chips in. It seems that, on the whole, mums don't like her, but dads do.

'My dad can't stand her!' I admit, giving up on any hope of a decent discussion about the ice caps.

'I think she's beautiful,' says Tasheika, who is pretty gorgeous herself.

'She hasn't got a single brain cell in her head,' pronounces Lissa, in a bored voice.

'That's not true!' I find myself springing to Alana de Silva's defence.

'Why are you defending her?' asks Lissa in surprise. 'You said in class you didn't want to be her.'

'I don't! But she's not stupid.'

'How do you know?'

Everyone is staring at me and I can feel myself going red. 'Well, she can't be, can she?' I say.

'Why not?' Lissa sounds as if she thinks *I'm* stupid and I go redder still.

'It stands to reason. She's come from nowhere and now she's really famous.'

'Big deal! Famous for making a fool of herself.'

With everyone watching and waiting for me to

reply, I can feel my skin tingling and I don't know what to say.

Dani tries to make a joke of it. 'Well, you've got to admit, for someone on the up and up she does seem to have a problem with falling down.'

Everyone laughs.

'And falling out of her clothes,' says Georgia with a grin.

'And falling in love!' sneers her friend who turns out to be called Zadie.

'And falling in with the wrong crowd,' says Lissa, joining in the competition.

'And falling out with people!' caps Dani and they all roll about laughing.

I feel like they're laughing at me as well as Alana de Silva.

'Now *you're* being stupid,' says Tash coldly, and her tone wipes the smirks off their faces.

'Sorry,' says Dani. 'I forgot she was your idol.'

'Sorry,' echoes Lissa. 'It's just that she's forever in the paper for falling over drunk or falling out with someone and getting into a fight . . .' Her voice fades away. I get the impression she's not used to apologizing.

'Really?' Tash gives her a withering look.

'Come on, Alice!' She walks away and I follow in her footsteps.

Tash is *so* brave to stand up for Alana de Silva against the others. I wish I could be as brave as her. Just like my sister Nikki, Tash isn't scared of anyone.

At the end of the school day I grab her by the arm before she dashes off.

'Thanks,' I say.

'What for?'

'Sticking up for me against the others at lunchtime.'

'It was nothing.'

'Yes, it was. I wish I could be as brave as you and stand up for what I believe in.'

'You do.' She looks at me oddly. 'Look what you were like today, going on and on and on about saving the planet.'

On and on and on. Was she bored by my speech too? But then she grins and I know she doesn't intend to be mean.

'They were way out of order anyway,' she says. 'I think Alana de Silva is amazing, don't you?' I smile back at Tash, glad that she's my friend.

'Um, I don't know. I have to admit, I don't really agree with her lifestyle. It all seems a bit shallow to me. I mean, there are far more important things to worry about in the world than the latest must-have shoes or bag –'

'Sorry, Alice! Got to go!' exclaims Tash suddenly, glancing at her watch.

And before I can mention the ice caps she's disappeared.

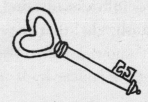

Chapter 10

The next morning I wait for ages for Tash at the bus stop. In the end I jump on a bus without her, scared I'll be late. Tash must've got on the next one because she appears in class just before the register is called. Miss Webb gives her a look though she doesn't say anything. I'm worried Tash'll be cross with me for not waiting, but she doesn't seem to mind.

Then I worry that she made herself late deliberately because she didn't want to travel in with me.

Today in PE we play netball. I played it at my last school, but I wasn't much good. I can feel Mrs Waters, the PE teacher, watching us closely so I try extra-hard, but still I never seem to get the ball.

At the end of the lesson she says, 'Well done,

everyone.' But I don't think she means me because she says, 'Nice work, Danielle,' and, 'Well played, Tasheika.' She doesn't say anything to me even though I'm standing right next to them. They're both really good in different ways. Tash is like a ballerina, leaping into the air to place the ball neatly inside the net; Dani's a whippet, racing round the court, always ready in the right place to receive the ball and feed it to the next person. Lissa's pretty good too.

I'm not sure I'll ever be any good at sport.

Next time we have PE we play hockey which none of us has played before. Mrs Waters tells us the positions and the rules and demonstrates some basic skills.

'First we will practise dribbling,' she says, which makes us all giggle, but it's not what you think. Basically, it's controlling the ball with the stick and it's harder than it sounds. When we've sort of mastered it (not me!), we get into twos and practise hitting the ball to each other and receiving it. You have to get down low and stop it. I practise with Dani and she's really good, but I keep missing the ball and have to go chasing up the field after it.

After a while Mrs Waters swaps us around. 'I think you two might be more evenly matched,' she says and partners Dani with Tash. She puts me with Nisha – she's not much good either.

Eventually, when Miss thinks we're all ready, we try a short game. Dani is outstanding, running rings round the rest of us.

'It's a bit like football,' she says happily as she comes back from scoring her third goal.

At the end of the lesson Mrs Waters makes us all sit down in the changing room. 'Right then, listen up,' she says. 'Every day next week there will be practices at lunchtime and after school for netball and hockey. At the end of the week I will pick the Year Seven teams. If you would like to be part of a team you must get your parents to sign one of these permission forms and you must turn up to each practice.'

'Lunchtimes *and* after school?' asks Tash, looking anxious.

'Lunchtimes for netball, after school for hockey,' says the teacher.

I don't think Tash is allowed to hang about after school; I've noticed she always nips off quickly. I thought we'd be getting the bus to and from school together every day, but it hasn't worked out like that. In the morning she's nearly always late, so now she's told me if she's not there to go without her, and at the end of the day she's out of the door as soon as the bell's gone.

But I've stopped worrying that it's me she's trying to avoid because at school we're always together. I really like Tash, she's so funny and she's kind as well. I like her best of everybody. I think she likes me best too.

Mrs Waters looks at her sternly. 'It shouldn't make any difference when the practices are, Tasheika. If you are committed to the team you will find time to attend. And that's what I'm looking for: commitment.'

'Yes, Miss,' says Tash meekly, but behind the teacher's back she pulls a face, crossing her eyes and sticking her tongue out of the side of her mouth like a gargoyle, which makes us all laugh. Mrs Waters turns round and eyes her suspiciously, but Tash smiles back at her, the picture of innocence, so she just tells us all to hurry up and get changed and disappears into her office.

'Are you trying out for the teams?' Tash asks me.

'I'm not sure . . .'

'I am!' says Dani. 'What about you, Lissa?'

'You bet!' she says. 'My mum was captain of the hockey team when she was here.'

I try to imagine Mrs Hamilton, immaculately dressed with her pearls round her neck and not a hair out of place, running around the school field brandishing a hockey stick. But then Tash says, 'I don't want to play hockey. I'm just going to try out for netball,' and we all stare at her in surprise.

'But you should!' says Dani. 'You were really good.'

'Yeah, come on, Tash. It would be great if we all got in,' says Lissa.

'I don't know . . .'

'Please, Tash,' says Dani, linking her arm through hers. 'It won't be any fun without you. And you too, Alice,' she adds as an afterthought.

Tash shrugs her shoulders. 'Oh, all right then! I probably won't be picked anyway.'

But she will. They all will. It's me that will be left on my own.

Mrs Waters appears at the door. 'Are you lot still here?' she says. 'Get a move on, you'll be late for your next lesson.'

'Did you know, Miss,' says Dani, 'Lissa's mum played hockey for this school?'

'Did you teach her, Miss?' asks Tash with interest.

Mrs Waters' neck elongates like an ostrich. 'How old do you think I am, Tasheika?'

Tash stares at her, trying to work it out. It's hard to tell with a teacher.

Actually, I think this might be what Miss Webb referred to in English as a 'rhetorical question'. That means the person who asks it might not really expect an answer. As Tash opens her mouth, I dig her in the ribs. 'Come on, we're late.'

Mrs Waters holds the door open for us and we all troop through.

'Bye, Miss,' says Tash.

'Bye, girls. See you at practice. I expect the Gang of Four to be there,' she says with smiley eyes, and we all chorus, 'We will!'

'I think she likes us,' says Tash, rubbing her ribs. 'What did you do that for?'

'You nearly put your foot in it.'

'How?'

'By telling her how old you thought she was.'

Tash looks puzzled. 'But she asked.'

Lissa rolls her eyes. 'Some things are meant to be kept secret. Like a lady's age.'

'Who says?'

'My mum.'

Tash frowns. 'My mum doesn't keep her age a secret. She's thirty-two.'

Dani gasps. 'Is that all? Mine's thirty-eight!'

'Mine's forty-five,' I admit. 'How old is yours, Lissa?'

'I don't know, it's a secret,' she explains patiently. 'But she's ancient.'

Tash giggles. 'No wonder Mrs Waters got mad when I asked her if she'd taught your mum. Why would you want to make a secret of your age? No secrets for the Gang of Four, hey?'

My heart plummets. Even Dani and Lissa look a bit surprised. Tash's face falls.

'Stupid thing to say!' she says. 'I suppose we've all got things we don't want people to know about.'

'I haven't!' says Dani quickly.

'Me neither,' says Lissa.

Everyone is looking at me. 'No secrets!' I say firmly.

'Nor me,' says Tash. 'So that's OK.'

We link arms and stroll off together to our next lesson. I've got a nice, warm, squishy feeling inside of me. I love being in a gang of four. It's twice as good as being in a gang of two, like Chloe and Emma the clones, who Dani has already rechristened collectively as Chlemma, and it's a hundred times better than being in a gang of one, like I expected to be.

But suddenly the nice, warm, squishy feeling inside of me solidifies into a cold block of ice. I've just thought of something.

If they get into the teams and I don't . . . I won't be one of the Gang of Four any more.

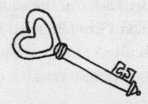

Chapter 11

My sister Nikki is always out. She's either working or she's 'out on the tiles' as Mum calls it, which is quite a funny concept if you think about it. It sort of fits in with Dad complaining that she's forever 'raising the roof'. It doesn't mean that Nikki is climbing about on the tops of buildings trying to make them higher. It means that she stays out late and gets into trouble and Mum and Dad, especially Dad, are always having a go at her about it. You can't blame them.

Tonight they're hard at it. She got in really late last night (what's new?) and Mum and Dad lay awake for ages worrying about her.

'Why don't I just move out and leave you in peace?' says Nikki. 'I could get a flat.'

'No,' says Mum.

'You must be joking,' says Dad.

'Why not? At least you could get a good night's sleep.'

'We wouldn't sleep a wink,' says Dad. 'We'd be worried sick you'd be out all night, up to no good.'

'That is *so* unfair!'

'You wouldn't eat properly,' says Mum.

'Of course I'd eat properly!'

'You haven't got time to look after yourself, Nikki. Anyway, I'd be concerned about you being on your own.'

'I wouldn't *be* on my own.'

'Who are you thinking of sharing with then?'

Pause. Then Nikki says defiantly, 'Greg.'

'That waste of space!' says Dad, and he and Nikki glare at each other.

'You've only known him two minutes!' says Mum, astounded.

'No, I haven't. I've been going out with him for ages, but there was no point in telling you because you never like my boyfriends –'

'How long is ages?' interrupts Dad.

'Three months.'

Dad rolls his eyes. 'That would be the three months you've been out till all hours, been brought home drunk, got thrown out of that nightclub for slapping someone and threatened with arrest . . .'

'She slapped me first!'

He carries on regardless, holding his hand up so we can see him ticking off the list of Nikki's misdemeanours on his fingers: '. . . wrote off your car, crashed *my* van . . .'

'They crashed into me! Stop doing that!' She slaps his hand down and growls at him, 'I knew he would never stand a chance with you. You and your stupid prejudices.'

'Loyalties, Nicola, not prejudices. Something you don't understand. He's leading you astray and –' he puts his face close to hers and repeats slowly, like he's imparting words of wisdom and she's too thick to get it – 'he's a waste of space.'

'Aaargh!' Nikki gives up, like she's lost for words. 'Tell him, Mum.'

'Maybe we should invite him round, Colin. Get to know him a bit. If our Nikki's serious about him . . .'

Dad looks as if he's going to explode. 'Over my dead body!'

'Don't tempt me,' mutters Nikki. She grabs her bag and goes out, slamming the door behind her. Seconds later we hear the sound of her car screeching off. She's got a new one, I forgot to say – same model, minus the dents and scratches.

Dad's still got his dents and scratches. He couldn't afford to replace his van. Nikki thinks that's the problem. She offered to buy him a new one but he refused point-blank.

Nikki's loaded. She's done so well since she left school. She's earning piles more than Dad and she's only got herself to look after.

That should make Dad proud.

It doesn't though.

He goes round telling anyone who'll listen that I go to Riverside Academy. But he never tells a soul what Nikki does for a living. Neither do I.

I told my new friends a lie. I do have a secret.

But it's not about me.

It's about Nikki.

Chapter 12

Nikki has decided she's definitely moving in with Greg. They've put down a deposit on a brand-new apartment in a flash new warehouse development, only it won't be ready for a few weeks. It's going to be a lot more peaceful round here without her and Dad at loggerheads all the time, that's for sure. But at least there's always something going on when Nikki's around.

All week we've got practices: lunchtimes, netball; after school, hockey. At breaktime on Monday Tash says, 'Let's eat our lunch now so we can be the first ones out to netball. Mrs Waters rates being on time *very* highly.'

'Good idea,' I say, pulling out my sarnies. I need all the help I can get to make this team. But Lissa's not very keen.

'Why not?' asks Tash.

'I'd prefer to eat my lunch at the proper time,' says Lissa in her best snooty voice.

'It's only for a week!' says Dani, but Lissa won't. She sits beside us looking cross while we eat our sandwiches. Then in French, the last lesson before lunch, Madame Dupré catches her wolfing down a banana on the quiet and gives her a lunchtime detention.

But as Lissa sits there struck dumb I realize something. Mrs Waters will never let her be in the team if she doesn't turn up for practice, no matter how good she is! And if she's got detention she won't be able to . . . Luckily, Tash jumps to her aid.

'It's not her fault, Madame!' she protests. 'She's got a medical condition.' Lissa looks at her in alarm. 'She's lacking in potassium,' explains Tash.

Only Tash could get away with it. But amazingly our French teacher believes her and lets Lissa off!

At netball I try my best, but it seems the harder I try the worse I get. Or maybe the gap is widening as everyone else gets better. It's the same in hockey. Mrs Waters is watching us like a hawk; she doesn't miss a trick. We all rush to change after school so we can be the first out again. She approves of that, you can tell.

Tash wins every time – she's super-fast. She can get changed in two seconds flat. After hockey training, she doesn't even bother to get out of her kit; she just tears straight off home as soon as the whistle blows.

By Friday lunchtime, at the end of netball practice, we're all knackered – even Dani. But Lissa looks the worst – she is grey with exhaustion.

'Are you all right?' I ask.

'Yes, why wouldn't I be?' she snaps back and I wonder what I've done to upset her.

'Moo-dy!' mouths Dani silently, and we leave her alone after that.

'Right, girls, there are so many good players in the year it's been really hard to pick a team,' says Mrs Waters and we all sit up. But then she adds, 'I will announce it on Monday together with the hockey team. I still have some decisions to make so this afternoon's practice is important.'

'I'm sorry, Miss, I can't come,' says Tash. We all stare at her in surprise.

'Why not?' Mrs Waters fixes her with a gimlet glare. 'I thought you were serious about making the team.'

'I am. But I've got the dentist after school.'

I wonder why she hadn't mentioned it before.

The teacher sighs disapprovingly and thrusts out her hand. 'Show me your appointment card.'

'I haven't got it with me.' Tash's eyes swivel away from the teacher's. I've seen her do that before, yesterday in fact, when she told Miss Webb she'd forgotten her English book with her homework in it. But I could see it there in her bag right next to me.

'Bring it on Monday,' orders Mrs Waters, looking cross.

At the end of school Tash shoots off as usual before I have the chance to speak to her. I wonder if her dentist appointment has put paid to her chances of getting picked and just for a fleeting second I find myself secretly hoping that it has. How mean is that? But I can't bear the thought of everyone being in the teams except me. I'm dreading Monday when we find out.

The weekend passes slowly. It would have been nice to do something with my new friends, but Dani says she's meeting up with mates from her old school and Lissa was so grumpy on Friday I didn't like to ask her what she was doing. I'd really love to spend time with Tash the most, but she always seems to be busy doing stuff with her mum. I think they must be really close.

Unless it's an excuse and she doesn't want to hang out with me.

On Saturday I end up ringing Austen, my safe bet, but even he says he's too busy to see me. He's in the middle of a project.

'Oh,' I say, disappointed. 'What are you doing?'

'An energy assessment on my house.'

I fall silent. Doesn't anyone want to spend time with me? Then Austen says, 'I could come over tomorrow and do one on yours if you want?'

I perk up a bit. 'Yes please.'

On Saturdays Dad disappears to his usual football match. Bedford Rovers are playing away today. He's been following the Rovers all his life; it's like his first love, his religion, his personal identity. Mum said they even had to plan their wedding for a day that the Rovers weren't playing.

She gets a bit fed up with it sometimes, so a couple of years ago he tried to involve us by taking us with him to a home match. It didn't work out at all. Dad got upset because Nikki was being eyed up by all the blokes and he kept warning them off. Mum got upset by the bad language they were using and she kept telling

69

them off. I got upset by the amount of fast food people were consuming and the number of non-biodegradable polystyrene containers they were dropping on the floor. I kept asking them if they knew how bad they were for our planet and would they like to pick them up and take them home. I can't believe I did that now! Some looked a bit surprised but ignored me; others bent down and picked them up and stuffed them into their pockets. One or two of them swore at me so Mum told them off too.

Nikki said we were all totally embarrassing and it was a stupid, boring game anyway. And Dad said, 'Never again!'

Dad goes on his own now. He meets up with his mates there, of course, but a lot of them take their sons or daughters with them nowadays.

Life is weird. Take Dani, for instance. She'd give anything to go and watch football with her dad, but she doesn't get a look in. It's not fair, is it?

Then I have a brilliant idea. Dani could go and watch the footie with *my* dad!

It's not that simple though. Dani may eat, sleep and breathe football, but she supports our other local team, West Park Wanderers, who are the Rovers' biggest rivals. And my dad hates the Wanderers with a vengeance.

But here's the really weird thing! My sister Nikki, who vowed she would never ever set foot inside a football ground again, is at this precise moment sitting in the Wanderers' stand, cheering them on.

Dad thinks she's doing it just to annoy him.

But she's not.

She's doing it for Greg.

Chapter 13

It's good to see Austen on Sunday. I'd forgotten how easy he is to be with. Boys might not be such good listeners as girls, but they're much more straightforward. Austen is never moody like Lissa, nor rushing off somewhere like Tash. And, unlike Dani, he's not obsessed with football.

He turns up with a clipboard and pen to record our energy consumption and walks around our house from room to room, switching off lights and appliances and turning down the thermostats on the radiators. It's an uphill struggle with my family. In Nikki's room alone, eleven appliances have been left on or are charging or on standby and she's not even out of bed yet. I call them out and Austen writes them all down.

'Main light, radiator, radio-alarm, heated rollers, hair straighteners . . .'

'Why would you want to curl and straighten your hair at the same time?'

'You don't do it at the same time . . . iPod, iPhone, bedside lamp, electric toothbrush, hairdryer, heated eye-mask thing . . .'

'What are you two doing?' Nikki sits up in bed and pulls her eye mask off, staring at us with bleary eyes.

'Making an inventory of how much energy you are wasting.'

'I'm not wasting energy, I'm conserving it.'

'How?'

'By sleeping. Now get lost, both of you.'

'But while you are sleeping do you realize how much electricity you are burning in this one room alone?' asks Austen politely.

Nikki groans. 'No, but I'm sure you're going to tell me.'

He does some quick calculations and informs her of the results, but she's gone back to sleep.

My parents are just as bad. Downstairs, Mum is unloading sheets and towels from the washing machine and about to put another wash on. Austen helpfully points out to her that it will work just as effectively on a lower temperature and she obligingly turns it down. Good old

Mum. She starts packing the sheets into the tumble dryer.

'Drying them outside in the fresh air is much better, ecologically,' I inform her. 'It's a lovely, breezy day.'

'Do it yourself then,' she says, dumping the wet sheets into my arms. 'I've got the dinner to see to.'

Austen disappears out the front to talk to my dad who's trying to mend the van. I peg the sheets out on my own (not an easy task) then go back into the kitchen where Mum is peeling a mountain of potatoes for the Sunday roast.

'Did you know that the rings on the hob can be turned down low and the vegetables will cook just as effectively?' I say, but she just tells me to give her a hand with the sprouts.

'How many food miles have these travelled?' I ask, looking doubtfully at the label on the net bag, but she says, 'Just get on with it, will you?'

She's a bit grumpy today so I don't tell her that she should turn the oven down too, where the chicken is roasting. I just do it myself when she's not looking.

When I've finished the sprouts I wander outside to find Austen. He's talking to dad's legs, which are sticking out from beneath the van. 'Your tyres are a bit flat,' I can hear him saying.

'They're fine,' answers Dad.

'Did you know that if you pump up your tyres properly you can save money on petrol?' persists Austen.

Dad doesn't reply so Austen repeats the question and Dad grunts.

After a while Austen makes another suggestion. 'Have you ever thought about buying an electric car?'

'No,' comes the answer but Austen doesn't give up that easily.

'They consume far less energy,' he informs him. 'Did you know that over a period of twenty years, pound for pound, it can be cheaper to –'

He's interrupted by the sound of something falling from beneath the van and a rude word from Dad, followed by another very, very rude word indeed. I decide to go back indoors.

What is wrong with everyone today?

To be fair, Mum does invite Austen to stay for dinner. His face lights up and he says, 'Is the chicken organic?' and she says, 'No,' so he says, 'No thank you, Mrs Grimes, I'm afraid I have to get home,' and she looks as if she might explode.

But he doesn't mean to be rude; it's just him. There is no way he would eat a chicken unless it had previously enjoyed a free-range, insect-foraging, pecking-round-the-yard life of bliss, like his do.

Anyway, it looks like he made the right decision. When we sit down to eat, it turns out that the chicken isn't cooked through. In fact, it's pink, the sort of shade Dad goes when he forgets to put sunscreen on.

'I'm not eating this!' says Nikki who's finally hauled herself out of bed. She takes a bite of roast potato instead and her face screws up with distaste. 'These are rock hard too.'

'I can't understand it, I cooked it the same as usual,' says Mum looking perplexed. Then her face clears. 'Alice, did you and that boy have a hand in this?'

When Mum calls Austen *that boy* I know she's cross.

'I turned the oven down a smidgeon,' I admit. 'Did you know that a few degrees lower can make a difference to –'

'Stop quoting him!' shrieks Mum.

'Who?' I say innocently.

'Old Earthy Penberthy. He's a blooming

know-all!' says Dad, poking morosely at his uncooked chicken leg.

'No, he's not!'

'Yes, he is,' chips in Nikki. 'Always banging on about the environment. He's boring! And he's making you boring too.'

'No, he isn't!' I protest. 'Just because you are superficial and only care about yourself, it doesn't mean that people who care about the environment are boring!'

But no one's listening. Outside, it's started raining. Mum swears under her breath and hauls herself up from the table. 'Give me a hand, Alice, my sheets are getting wet!'

Some people are never grateful.

It's not easy trying to save the planet in my family. I'll be glad to get back to school tomorrow and be with my new friends again.

At least they don't think I'm boring.

I hope.

Chapter 14

Monday morning. D-Day.

Or should I say T-Day, as in Teams Day?

Everyone's excited. Well, everyone who's tried out, that is. Some girls Dani calls the Barbies are too obsessed with their appearance to chase a ball around. Though surprisingly Georgia was up for it and she's a Barbie. Some girls Tash calls the Profs (as in professors) are too intellectual, and a few just don't care. But most of us would sell our grannies to get picked, including me. (Sorry, Granny!) *Especially* me. Because I'm one of the Gang of Four and the other three are bound to get in. Though I know I won't.

Miss Webb talks to us about the School Council in form time, but I find it hard to take in. It's double PE first lesson.

We cram into the changing rooms, the whole year group, and it's so noisy! All around me people are saying things like, 'I won't get in!' and 'I won't be picked!' and everyone is busy reassuring everyone else that of course they will, but I'm too nervous to speak. I feel like a can of fizzy drink that's been shaken up and is ready to explode. Then Mrs Waters walks in with a list in her hand and everyone falls silent.

Miss smiles at us sympathetically. 'I know you're all dying to know, so I'm going to put you out of your misery straight away. These are the people I have selected for the hockey team . . .'

Lissa, Tash, Dani and I grab each other's hands and squeeze tight.

'Danielle Jarvis.' A cheer goes up and Dani beams from ear to ear.

'Tasheika Campbell.' Tash shrieks and jumps up and down with excitement.

We grip hands again as Mrs Waters continues to run through the list. Beside me, Lissa has her eyes closed. At last we hear, 'Melissa Hamilton,' and Lissa's eyes shoot open. The other two beam at her.

'You're next!' says Tash but she's wrong. I'm not

next. I'm not picked at all. When the last name is called, the others turn to me, their faces sad.

'I knew I wouldn't be!' I say flippantly as if I'm not bothered. But inside all my fizz has evaporated, leaving me flat and empty.

'Don't worry,' says Tash. 'There's still the netball team.'

I don't want to hold hands with the others this time. Instead I fold my arms, digging my nails into my palms. But it makes no difference. I don't get into the netball team either.

Dani does. And Lissa. And Tash.

'I'm sorry!' she says and flings her arms round me.

'I don't mind,' I say. 'Well done, you!'

I may be no good at sport, but I'm really good at acting. She grins at me, relieved I've taken it so well. But she can't see the white nail marks on my palms. As the blood courses back into them, they are turning an angry red.

'The team members are not written in stone. You all have to earn your places. I'm going to be watching you all the time. If anyone is slacking they will lose their place to another member of Year Seven. *Blah, blah, blah-di-blah* . . .' The teacher's voice drones on, but I've stopped listening.

What a shame. You didn't make the teams, did you? taunts a nasty little voice inside my head.

So? I say to myself crossly. *What difference does it make?*

It makes a big difference, insists the mean little voice. *You're not one of the Gang of Four any more.*

We go outside to play netball for the rest of the lesson and Mrs Waters divides us into teams. I'm centre opposite Tash. She's in a giddy, silly mood, pleased with herself for getting into both squads, and she's not concentrating. I'm the opposite. Determined to show everyone (especially me!) I'm just as good as her, I find myself playing like a person possessed.

At the end of the game Mrs Waters says, 'Well played, Alice!' and for a moment I'm pleased. Then I remember she never chose me and I feel let down all over again.

Lissa must be a mind-reader because she touches my arm as we're walking off the court and says, 'You were brilliant!' and I say, 'Thanks.'

She looks as if she's about to say something else, but then Tash catches up with us and thumps me on the back.

'Wow!' she says. 'You ran rings round me!' and Lissa walks away.

When we get back into the changing rooms Mrs Waters says, 'One more thing. It's time to pick the captains. Team captain is a very responsible position. I want you to think very carefully about who would be the best person to lead each team. I will take up to three nominations for each position and no, Tasheika, before you ask, you cannot nominate yourself.'

Everyone laughs, including Tash, loudest of all. She's got nothing to worry about; everyone loves happy, smiley Tasheika. Someone's bound to nominate *her*.

Normally it would be me, but somehow I'm not in the mood. She doesn't need me anyway; she's surrounded by people who want to be her friend.

'So, your choice for netball captain?' asks Mrs Waters and hands shoot up.

Tash's name is the first to be called.

Dani's is the second.

Lissa's is the third.

'That's enough,' says Mrs Waters. 'Let's take nominations for the hockey captain now.' And hands shoot up again.

This time Dani's name is the first to be called.

Lissa's is the second.

And Tash's is the third.

They stand out the front, looking proud. The Gang of Three.

Now I feel *really* left out. I'd give anything to be standing out there at the front with them. Instead, I'm sitting on my own at the back of the changing room.

We choose the hockey captain first. Mrs Waters sends the nominees out and says, 'Right then, girls. One vote each. Who wants to vote for Danielle?'

I put up my hand without thinking. So does everyone else. Dani is by far the best hockey player in the year. Probably in the school!

'That's it then, unanimous,' says Mrs Waters and calls them back in. When she announces that Dani's the captain, I can't help noticing a flicker of surprise in Lissa's eyes. Just a little shiver and it's gone.

She thought she was going to be hockey captain. Of course she did. Her mum was, and she thought she would be too. Poor Lissa. She's used to getting what she wants, I guess.

I'd been so busy feeling sorry for myself it hadn't occurred to me till now that there were two positions and three people up for them.

Somebody else was going to be very disappointed.

'Right then, netball captain next,' says the teacher. 'I'm sorry, but you can't vote for Danielle this time. Melissa and Tasheika, outside please.'

They go back out, Lissa looking a bit tense, Tash grinning and doing a silly phone hand to make us all laugh.

Only I don't feel like laughing.

'Who wants to vote for Tasheika?' asks Mrs Waters.

She counts the votes.

'And who wants to vote for Melissa?'

She counts again. It's easy this time. Lissa's nice but she can be a bit moody and a tad superior. There's only one vote for her. Everyone voted for Tash instead. Kind, friendly Tash, the most popular girl in Year Seven. Everyone except me, her best friend. Only nobody notices, except Mrs Waters, because I'm sitting at the back.

'Right then, Tasheika it is,' she says briskly.

Lissa and Tash come back into the changing rooms, looking nervous. Mrs Waters announces that Tash has won and Lissa shakes hands with her.

'Congratulations,' she says nicely, with a small, tight smile.

'Thanks,' says Tash, with a big, beaming grin. Dani grabs her hand and thrusts it triumphantly high in the air and everyone cheers. Nearly everyone.

Two happy captains. The Gang of Two.

'Off you go now, everyone,' says Mrs Waters. 'Not you, Dani and Tasheika. I want a word with you.'

I follow Lissa out of the changing rooms. 'Well done for getting in the teams,' I say to her.

'Thanks,' she answers. But, like me, she doesn't look as though she feels much like celebrating.

Chapter 15

Mrs Waters had asked to see her new captains at lunchtime, so Lissa and I hang out together. It's quiet, just the two of us. Normally you can hear the Gang of Four across the dining hall as we all try to get a word in edgeways, but today neither of us feels like talking. I don't even feel much like eating.

'Don't you want that chocolate bar?' asks Lissa, eyeing my lunchbox. I shrug so she helps herself. I think her mum disapproves of sugary treats. She disapproves of most things if you ask me.

Afterwards we go out on the field and, as we sit down, Dani and Tash come out of the changing rooms together, looking bright and happy. The Golden Girls. I'm *so* jealous. It's like the sun's blazing down on them alone, leaving

Lissa and me in the shade. They don't even notice us, they're so busy chatting.

Mrs Waters follows them out. 'Hurry up and get your lunch,' we hear her say and they shout, 'Bye, Miss!' and race straight past us. We watch them disappearing into the dining hall.

'I think you should've got into the hockey team instead of Tash,' says Lissa. 'You made all the practices. She didn't.'

'She's better than me.'

'No she's not. You're just as good as she is. You just don't show off as much.'

'Thanks,' I say, taken aback. Because I know it's not true.

But then, because she's being so nice, I blurt out, 'I voted for you for captain.'

She looks so grateful it surprises me. 'For the hockey team? Thanks, Ali!'

I remember the unanimous vote for Dani. 'For both,' I say, crossing my fingers against the lie.

After that we talk and talk and talk.

Today I learn something. You can't always tell what people are like from appearances. I don't think Lissa is half as confident as she makes out. She's worried about telling her mum that she didn't get hockey captain. It's sort of expected of her, she explains, what with her mother being it when she was at school and Lissa's brother being captain of his rugby team.

It must be hard to have to follow in someone's footsteps like that. I've got something to thank my sister for after all. My parents would never want me to be like Nikki, especially my dad. I don't want to be like her either. I'd rather be boring than embarrassing.

I think.

Question: Would you rather everyone thought you were really, really embarrassing? Or really, really boring?

Help! I push this thought firmly out of my mind for the time being. This is not about me, it's about Lissa. 'You don't have to be like your mum,' I point out to her.

'You don't know her,' she says gloomily, but I do. I know her enough to understand she's one of those pushy, competitive mums who wants their child to be the best at everything. I mean, my mum's pleased if I do well. But she's pleased for *me*, not for her – that's the difference.

I never thought I'd say this, but I feel a bit sorry for Lissa.

'You don't have to be a hockey captain just

because she was,' I insist. 'You can do something else to make her proud of you.'

'Like what?'

I think for a moment. Then I remember what Miss Webb was talking about in form-time this morning. 'You could be a rep on the School Council. You'd be really good at that.'

Lissa raises her eyes to mine. 'D'you reckon?'

'Yes, I do.'

'So would you. Look what you're like when you bang on about the environment.'

'Do I?'

'What?'

'Bang on about the environment?'

'All the time.'

My heart sinks. Austen bangs on about the environment all the time and Nikki says he's boring. I knew it. Everyone thinks I'm boring too.

But then her face lights up. 'We could do it together! Miss Webb said each year group could elect two people to represent them,' and she sounds all excited and my heart leaps back to its proper place.

At that moment, Dani and Tash come out of lunch together, arm in arm.

'Here they come, the Captains of Year Seven,' remarks Lissa, and now her voice sounds a bit flat and hollow.

'They'd make good reps too,' I observe, but my voice sounds a bit flat and hollow as well.

As Tash spots us and waves, and they head over towards us, Lissa turns to me. 'Let's do it, Ali!' she says urgently. 'You and me. But don't tell them!'

Then the bell goes, and she gets to her feet and tucks her arm through mine. And the four of us all stroll into school together.

On my way home from school that day, I'm feeling really miserable. It's been a rubbish day. Not only did I fail to make the teams but also I've been disloyal to Tash. I owe a lot to my ditzy, glitzy, fun-loving best friend. It's because of her more than anyone that school is OK and I'm not sitting on my own like I thought I would be.

Yet today I'd turned my back on her and voted for Lissa instead. I feel like I've betrayed her.

I knew why I'd done it. I was jealous.

And now Lissa and I would be putting ourselves forward as form reps and I haven't told Tash that either. I sat by her all afternoon and she never knew anything was wrong. She was just perfectly normal, getting on with her work, sharing my thesaurus, borrowing my felt tips. When Grumpy Griffiths asked me a question in maths and I didn't know the answer, Tash wrote it on her rough book for me so I didn't look stupid.

As soon as the bell went, I'd turned to her and said urgently, 'Let's do something this weekend. Just you and me.' Suddenly I really wanted to get everything off my chest. I wanted to tell her I hadn't voted for her and that I was sorry. And I wanted to tell her about standing for the School Council with Lissa. Because she'd understand, I knew she would. If only I could explain.

But she'd looked at me in surprise and said, 'I don't know . . . I might be busy. I don't know. My mum . . .' And it was obvious she didn't want to see me; she was just making excuses.

So I'd said quickly, 'It's OK, some other time,' and she'd said, 'Definitely!' and the relief on her face was plain to see. And, even though she'd given me her special hug before she'd dashed off at the end of the day, I'd felt like crying.

I still feel horrible – all confused and churned-up inside. Angry and let down and guilty all at the same time.

'How did you get on?' Mum asks before I even get through the front door.

'What do you mean?' Though I know exactly what she means. I dump my bags and go into the lounge where the television is blaring, and flop on to the sofa beside Nikki. She's snipping split ends from her hair with nail scissors and her eyes are going crossed with the effort. Mum follows me in, her face aglow, like she's swallowed a light bulb.

'Don't keep us in suspense. Did you get in the teams?'

'Nope.'

The light bulb goes out. 'Never mind,' she says sympathetically. 'Better luck next time.'

'Sport's overrated,' says Nikki, uncrossing her eyes. 'Who wants to get hot and sweaty chasing a ball around, anyway?'

'You did,' I remind her. Because, let's face it, my sister is not just beautiful, is she? She's bright, talented, got a great voice and, oh yeah, she's good at sport as well. She and Tash really have got a lot in common. Mum sits down in the armchair and we all stare blankly at *Blue Peter* on the television.

After a while, Nikki taps me on the knee with the scissors.

'You. Me. Tonight. Girly night in together.'

'Is that supposed to cheer me up?'

'You could do with a makeover,' she says and grabs hold of my ponytail and pretends to cut it off. I push her away.

'Are you going somewhere?' I ask Mum.

'Looks like.' She winks at Nikki. Then, as my dad walks through the door from work, she jumps to her feet and pushes him back out. 'Don't take your coat off, Colin, we're going out.'

Sooooo subtle.

Not long afterwards Nikki disappears and comes back with my favourite nibbles – parsnip crisps, samosas, onion bhajis and iced cupcakes. Plus cartons of juice, a bottle of schnapps and a bottle of vodka.

'What are these for?' I ask.

'Cocktails. Non-alcoholic for you, Sex on the Beach for me. You need your five a day,' she says cheerfully, mixing one part cranberry and orange and three parts schnapps and vodka into a cocktail shaker for herself. I pour orange juice, cranberry juice and mango into a glass and sip it cautiously. It's delicious. I help myself to a samosa and feel myself cheering up. Slightly.

But then her phone rings (what a surprise!) and

she wanders away, yakking. She's gone for ages. 'That was Greg,' she explains unnecessarily, coming back into the room.

'Are you going out?'

'No,' she says. 'I told him, I'm spending a night in with my little sister.'

'He's going to love me!' I say sarcastically.

'Yes, he is,' she replies with a grin. 'He's on his way over now.'

And so finally I get to meet Greg, the current love of my sister's life. The man Dad said was never to darken our doorstep.

Chapter 16

When the bell rings I jump up to open the door. This is the first time I've met Greg in the flesh, and he is every bit as hot as I thought he would be (Nikki's boyfriends always are). He is sooo big and looks like he works out. Plus he's got close-cropped hair, brown eyes, designer stubble and perfect white teeth. Yep, he ticks all the boxes all right. But, even though they've put down a deposit on a flat together, we've been here before and I'm not holding my breath.

Nikki always goes out with good-looking guys. Let's face it: she could have anyone she wanted with her looks. But all too often that's all they turn out to be — all looks, no substance, like cardboard cut-outs, and before long she gets bored. Or, worse still, they're up themselves: flaky, mean, moody or more obsessed with their appearance than she is. Either way she dumps them.

And all of them, needless to say, are totally uninterested in her nerdy kid sister.

But Greg's face lights up when he sees it's me at the door and he says, 'Hi, you must be Alice,' like I'm exactly who he was hoping to see. 'I've heard all about you!' he adds and I can't help noticing how his eyes crinkle up when he smiles.

He gives Nikki a kiss and a hug without making a meal of it (a tick in my book) and then sits down on the sofa. Nikki gives him a drink and he turns his attention back to me.

'So?' he says.

'So what?'

'You didn't make the teams then?'

I gasp. Go for the jugular, why don't you? But his eyes are warm and sympathetic.

'How do you feel about that?'

'Jealous.'

Why did I say that? There is something about this man that demands an honest response.

He nods. 'And?'

I swallow. 'Left out. No good. Rubbish.'

He winces. 'I know what that feels like.'

'You?' I say in disbelief.

His eyebrows lift. 'Oh yeah. It's happened to me loads. Still does. The boss chooses a team from the squad each game. Sometimes I don't get picked. Believe me, that hurts.' His face is serious. He's not making it up, I can tell.

Greg plays for West Park Wanderers. It's rumoured that this year he might get into the England squad. He's really good. But sometimes even he doesn't get selected.

I stare at him in surprise. 'How do you deal with that?'

He shakes his head. 'No one's got a divine right to a place in a team. You've got to earn it. Or get out and do something else.'

'Like what?'

'I don't know. You could do anything. Nikki says you're dead clever.'

'No I'm not . . .' I say automatically, but he just carries on.

'There are loads of things you could be good at. You've just got to find the right one. Me, I'm not much good at anything except football. So I just try harder. I train, work out, raise my game, lay off the booze . . .' He stares thoughtfully at the glass in his hand then raises it to his lips and tosses it back.

The next second he's coughing and spluttering like mad. Eyes popping and gasping for air, he falls to the floor and we jump up in alarm.

But then he starts twitching, like an enormous floppy fish in its death throes, and moans weakly, 'I need oxygen, I'm dying! Nikki, give me the kiss of life!' and we burst out laughing.

'Flaming Nora, Nikki!' he groans as we pull him to his feet. 'What are you trying to do? Finish me off?'

'Stop making such a fuss, you wimp,' says Nikki.

'Wimp! Do you know how strong this drink is, Nik? I thought it was fruit juice.'

'It is! With a dash of vodka and schnapps.'

'A dash! More like a crateful!'

He's laughing now, his eyes crinkling up again. He is so attractive. No wonder Nikki likes him.

Dad would like him too if he got to know him, even if he does play for the Wanderers. He thought Greg was the one leading Nikki astray but he's wrong. Greg is the sensible one.

Greg is the best boyfriend Nikki has ever had.

Chapter 17

We did it! Lissa and I are on the School Council together! We got voted in as reps by the whole of Year Seven! And we weren't the only ones who stood. Georgia and Zadie did as well and a couple of Profs and some girls from other classes, but *we* got in. I felt so proud when more people put their hands up for us in assembly than for anyone else and I know Lissa did too. It felt like the sun was blazing down on me for once, making me hot with happiness.

But back in class storm clouds were gathering. Georgia and Zadie were put out, obviously, but I don't mean them. I'm talking about two great big cumulonimbuses called Dani and Tash. I've never seen them so grumpy.

'Why didn't you tell us you were standing?' demands Tash, looking hurt.

'Yeah, I thought we weren't going to have any secrets from each other?' says Dani.

'It wasn't like that!' I say, but it was.

'It wasn't a secret,' explains Lissa. 'We only made up our minds to go for it last thing on Friday and you'd dashed off as usual. Then it was voting first thing this morning.'

She's lying. We'd decided to put ourselves forward last Monday when the other two had been made captains, but we'd kept it quiet for a whole week. Even though they don't know that, Dani and Tash exchange a look.

'We didn't have a chance to tell you in school,' I lie too. I didn't expect them to be this upset. 'And you said you were going to be busy at the weekend, remember?'

Tash's eyelids flicker. She remembers all right. 'Still,' she says sulkily, 'you could've picked up the phone.'

'I did! I rang you Saturday *and* Sunday but you didn't answer. You never do!'

That bit was true anyway. Lissa's eyes open wide with surprise. I hadn't told her that in a fit of conscience I'd tried to phone Tash to confess. Tash doesn't say anything.

'You're *always* busy at weekends,' Lissa points out. 'Both of you.'

'We weren't leaving you out!'

'It's OK,' says Tash flatly. But it isn't. I can feel all my happiness draining away. Why hadn't I told her last week?

Because Lissa had told me not to, that's why.

Because I was all mixed up.

And, if I'm honest, because I didn't want Tash and Dani muscling in on the act and whipping our prize away from us.

Now I feel really ashamed.

'I'll ask Miss Webb if we can vote again. I'll nominate you. You can be rep. Or Dani.'

Lissa looks at me in alarm. She wanted to be rep. So did I. But I didn't want Dani and Tash to feel left out. Especially Tash. She was so nice to me when I started Riverside. She's always nice to me.

'It wasn't meant to be a secret,' I say desperately.

'It's all right,' says Dani, shrugging. 'I don't want to be rep anyway. I haven't got time.'

'Me neither,' echoes Tash, but she still sounds forlorn. 'Just don't keep anything else from us, yeah?'

'I won't.'

'No more secrets. Promise?'

'Promise,' I say in relief and give her a hug. 'I'm really sorry.'

'It's OK. We're the Gang of Four, remember? The No Secrets Club.' Her stern face softens into her familiar smile and my world lights up again.

Briefly. But soon the cloud comes back.

I can't blame Tash and Dani this time. This is my own personal cloud, my guilty conscience that's blocking the sun from me. No one else seems to notice, but it's nearly always there, hovering over me. One day it will burst open, right on top of my head, and then everyone will know.

I have got a secret.

A big one.

I want to tell my friends, I really do. But the longer I keep it hidden the harder it is to do.

The trouble with secrets is they're like volcanoes. They're buried out of sight and you can try and forget about them, but they'll never go away. They're always bubbling away underground, threatening to erupt, letting off steam occasionally to remind you they're still there.

And one day you know, without a shadow of a doubt, that your own personal volcano will spew out its secret and sweep all your lovely new friends away with it.

Chapter 18

School has settled into a routine. I definitely don't feel like a new girl any more. There are a few kids in the class I'm still a bit wary of, like Georgia and her friends Zadie and Chantelle who think they know it all, but I try to keep out of their way. Dani nicknamed them the Barbies at first because she thought they were so obsessed with their appearance they were total airheads, but it turns out Georgia is a really good hockey player. She's still scary though.

It helps being mates with Tash and Dani and Lissa. I was worried that not being in the teams with them would make a difference, but it doesn't seem to have so far. They've only played one hockey match in school time, which they won. (Or which Dani won – she ran rings round the opposition apparently and I wish I could have seen it!) They played one away netball match too after school, but Tash missed it because she went home sick in the middle of the afternoon. Anyway, now Lissa and I are the reps on the School Council I don't mind so much. We're still the Gang of Four and the No Secrets Club, as Tash calls us.

If only she knew.

We sit together in class, Tash and me in front, Dani and Lissa behind, always in the same seats at the back. Even when we swap rooms we automatically take up the same positions, unless we're in the science lab or the IT room or in PE, obviously. I love sitting next to Tash. You never know what to expect next. She brings out the fun part of me. The part that is hidden deep down underneath serious Alice. Maybe I buried it deliberately to show I was different from Nikki.

We're all different, the four of us, but we get on really well. Most of the time. Except . . .

Lissa can be a touch moody.

Dani can be a tad anti-girly.

Tash can be a little scatty.

And I can't help worrying that they think I'm a bit boring.

Or a lot boring.

Tash can be lot scatty, actually. I'm not being mean, she's still my best friend, but it's true. Like, she's always late for school. She manages to avoid detention. Just. This morning she's the last one in as usual, slipping into the seat beside me just as Miss Webb starts the register. The teacher shakes her head.

'Try getting up a little earlier, Tasheika.'

'Yes, Miss,' says Tash meekly, but everyone knows tomorrow she'll be late again. It's weird because it's obvious she loves school.

Anyway, she's back in Miss Webb's good books straight away because we've got English first and Tash's hand is up and down like a yo-yo, answering questions.

It's the same in the next lesson, maths. Even Grumpy Griffiths likes her. I'm terrified of answering a question in maths in case I get it wrong and he gives me one of his ghoulish glares. His head looks like a skull. But Tash isn't scared of him at all. When she gives a wrong answer, she doesn't care, she just works it all out again and this time she gets it right. Grumpy Griffiths nods approvingly at her.

'Tasheika Campbell. Ir-re-pressible,' he intones in his gravelly, graveyard voice.

Tash giggles. 'That means I can't be pressed. I can't be ironed!' she informs the rest of us and we all laugh out loud, even our maths teacher, which is quite scary because his jaw drops open to reveal large yellow teeth like tombstones and his shoulders shake so much I think his head's going to fall off.

Today, at breaktime, Tash is holding forth about the new label Alana de Silva is wearing. I would usually join in with the chat, but this morning I just wish she'd stop going on about it.

'You're obsessed!' I say in the end. 'You must have spent the whole weekend reading celebrity magazines.'

'No, I didn't!' says Tash indignantly.

'Everyone else did,' says Dani, looking resigned, and I know how she feels. Sometimes I despair.

'Well, *I* didn't!' repeats Tash, but I don't believe her. I often wonder what she gets up to at weekends. Being as she never wants to meet up with me.

Thinking about this makes me grumpy and I hear myself saying, 'Can't you see there are more important things to worry about than what Alana de Silva is wearing?' But then I wish I hadn't because Tash starts to look cross.

'*Like?*' she asks pointedly.

'Football,' says Dani, and everyone laughs, including Tash, her good humour restored.

'Um, not exactly what I had in mind,' I say, relieved an argument has been avoided. But, I have to say, Dani's obsessed too. She's a total football fanatic (which is where the word *fan* comes from incidentally) and she spends her life following the Wanderers, even though she doesn't get to many of the matches any more, being as her dad's not around much.

I should introduce her to Greg. But I can't. If she meets Greg, she'll meet my sister. And I don't want that to happen.

I wish I'd told everyone about Nikki at the beginning. It's too late now.

Chapter 19

'Dani, why didn't you go to a mixed school?' asks Tash one day.

'I wanted to,' says Dani, 'but my mum sent me here so I'd make friends with girls. She's worried that I'm too much of a tomboy. I only agreed because Riverside's got the best reputation for sport for miles around.'

'But if you'd gone to a mixed school you could have played football,' Lissa points out.

Dani shakes her head. 'I doubt it. They're not supposed to discriminate now against girls, but they still do. I'd never have got a game. At least this way . . .' Her voice breaks off suddenly as if she's said more than she intended and we all stare at her.

'At least this way what?'

She takes a deep breath and grins at us all. 'At least this way I get to play hockey and netball and hang out with you guys too! You're the first girl mates I've ever had.'

Aahh! Dani's great. I make a list in my head of the reasons why I rate her so much.

1. She's her own person.
2. She doesn't gossip.
3. She's not afraid to be different.
4. She's funny.
5. She says what she thinks.
6. She's an excellent hockey captain.
7. She's really encouraging to everyone.
8. She always finds time to help you with your game.

Not like Tash.

I don't mean that nastily. I just mean that, even though Tash is netball captain, she's not committed to the sport like Dani is to hockey.

Like this afternoon, at the end of the day when we're all filing back into the changing room from PE Dani, focused as usual, says, 'Please, Miss, can the netball team stay on and practise?'

They all start pleading, 'Yes, Miss! Can we, Miss? Please?' All except Tash who says, 'I can't! I'm not allowed.'

'No one is allowed,' says Mrs Waters. 'Not today, anyway. I have to give your parents twenty-four hours' notice if you're staying behind at the end of the day. You can have an after-school practice tomorrow though, if you want to,' and she disappears into her office to get the forms.

Everyone cheers. Everyone except for Tash who's looking a bit worried.

'What's up?' I ask.

'I can't stay after school tomorrow either.'

'Why not?' asks Dani.

'I've got stuff to do.'

'What sort of stuff?'

'For my mum.'

'Tell her you're busy,' says Lissa, sounding annoyed.

'It's not that simple . . .'

'You're the captain, remember?' says Lissa and now her voice is sour. 'You're supposed to be in charge.'

At that moment Mrs Waters comes out of her office clutching a wad of forms.

'I can't make it tomorrow either, Miss,' says Tash. The rest of the team groans. I hold my breath, scared that she's going to get into trouble, but Mrs Waters just sighs.

'Don't worry, it's not as if it's a scheduled practice.' Her eyes dart from one face to the next and settle on me. 'Alice? What about you? Can you take Tasheika's place tomorrow after school?'

My heart flutters like a butterfly trapped inside my chest. Is this my chance to get in the team? I can't do that to Tash.

'Please, Alice!' everyone pleads. Everyone except Tash who is staring hard at the ground.

'Um . . . yeah. If it's OK with you, Tash.'

'It's fine,' she mutters, refusing to meet my eye. 'Can I go now?'

'Of course,' says Miss Waters, eyeing her curiously, and Tash grabs her bag and her clothes and dashes off for the bus without even stopping to change.

Dani stares after her in surprise. 'What's the hurry?'

'Got to get home quick to read more celebrity mags,' remarks Lissa innocently and we all laugh. But then I feel bad. Because maybe it wasn't such an innocent remark after all. I think Lissa genuinely feels she would've made a better captain than Tash.

OK. Maybe she would.

But Tash is still my best mate.

Chapter 20

This weekend I'm going to Lissa's house for the first time.

On Friday I asked Tash if she wanted to do something, but she's busy as usual.

'What are you doing?' I say, hurt that she never seems to want to spend time with me out of school.

'Going shopping with my mum,' she says, but I'm not sure I believe her. That mean little voice starts off inside my head again.

Nobody wants to spend that much time with their mum.

Maybe she's cross with you for taking her place at netball practice? Maybe she's got a secret friend she prefers to be with instead of you?

Don't be silly, I say to myself firmly. *Tash doesn't do secrets. None of us do. We're the No Secrets Club, remember?*

Then the mean little voice says, *But* you've *got a secret.*

Oh dear, I don't want to think about it.

'What about you, Dani – do you want to do something this weekend?' I ask. At least she gives me an honest answer.

'No thanks. I'm seeing my mates.'

'Who?'

'Sean, Ryan, Luke . . .'

'Boys,' I say flatly.

'Yep. Plus Vikram, Nathan, Marvyn, Alex . . .'

'Are you in a gang?' asks Tash.

'A gang?' Dani frowns. 'Course not. We just meet up and kick a football around together.'

Naturally. What else would you expect Dani to be doing on a Saturday? She'd either be watching a ball or kicking one around.

'I know a boy called Marvyn who's a good footballer,' says Tash thoughtfully.

Then Lissa says, 'You can come over to mine if you want.'

I hesitate. 'What about your mum?'

'What about her?'

'She might not want you to be friends with me.'

Dani looks puzzled. 'Why not? Everybody's mum would want her daughter to be friends with you.'

I'm not sure this is a compliment. 'What do you mean?'

'You're nice . . . neat . . . sensible . . . hard-working . . . and . . .'

Boring. I was right; it's not a compliment.

'. . . fun to be with . . .' continues Tash who can read my face, but it's too late. 'Why wouldn't her mum like you?'

'She means because her dad swore at my mum on the first day of school,' explains Lissa. 'It's OK, Ali, nobody noticed you, just your dad.'

This is meant to make me feel better but actually it makes me feel worse. Of course nobody noticed me. Why would they? Who's going to notice boring Alice?

On Saturday, when I go over to Lissa's, I'm feeling a bit bad about Austen and a conversation I'd had with him the night before.

'D'you want to go to the cinema tomorrow afternoon?' he'd asked.

'The cinema?' It's not the sort of thing we normally do.

'I'll pay,' he said quickly.

'It's not that . . .'

'It's a brilliant film,' he said. 'It's called

Destruction. I've just read up about it online. It's about this boy and this girl and they're struggling for survival. Mankind is about to be wiped out because of war and pollution and the exploitation of natural resources and they've got seven days to save the world . . .'

'I can't . . .'

'It's got, you know, other stuff in it too.'

'What stuff?'

'You know . . . romantic stuff. Boy-girl stuff. Love and that . . .' He'd sounded a bit embarrassed and it had made me giggle.

'I can't, Austen. I'm sorry.'

'It's all right.'

'I would, but I've already arranged to see my friend Lissa.'

'Not a problem.' His voice was clipped now, like he'd suddenly remembered he had other things to do.

'We'll catch up soon . . .' I said, but he'd put the phone down.

I'd love to have gone to the cinema with him. The film sounded brilliant. But I'd already promised Lissa I would go round to hers and one thing I would never be is a flaky friend, the sort who drops you if they get a better offer.

Anyway, I was curious to see the house Lissa lived in.

It turns out to be tall and posh, like Mrs Hamilton, and it stands behind a waist-high brick wall topped by spiky ornamental railings, presumably to keep the riff-raff out. Outside, the flashy sports car is standing guard in its designated parking space, looking as if it has far more right to be here than I do. I glance down at my jeans and the T-shirt that Nikki picked out for me to wear and wish I'd dressed up a bit more. And now I'm frightened to ring the doorbell in case Lissa's mother answers it and recognizes me as the girl who belongs to Scary, Sweary, White-Van Man.

But it's OK, the door opens anyway. Mrs Hamilton must have been watching out for me. She smiles down at me approvingly.

'You must be Alice, Melissa's friend,' she says, holding the door open wide. 'I've heard all about you. Do come in.'

Not quite all, I think as I step into the hallway. Inside, the house is even bigger than it looks from outside. I look around in amazement. It's like one of those houses from the homes-and-gardens magazines that I've flicked through in the doctor's waiting room.

Through open doorways I catch glimpses of beautiful rooms: a drawing room with deep leather sofas and floor-to-ceiling bookcases; a shiny, chrome kitchen that looks as if it's never been used; a dining room with the table already set for dinner with plates, glasses and napkins, like the five-star restaurant we went to for my grandparents' golden wedding. There are bowls of sweet-smelling flowers everywhere, classical music is wafting from the lounge and the whole house is immaculate.

I wish I'd gone to the cinema with Austen instead. This is far too posh for me.

Then Lissa appears at the top of the stairs and she's wearing torn jeans and exactly the same T-shirt as me and her eyes widen and she says, 'Snap!' and we all laugh, even her mum.

'Do go up!' says Mrs Hamilton and so I bound upstairs into Lissa's room and, OK, it's bigger than mine and she's got her own TV and computer and there's no Ikea furniture like I've got in my room, but actually it's not that different. There are posters on the walls and books and clothes and mugs and plates and hair-stuff and homework strewn around and it's MESSY! Much messier than mine. I plonk myself down on a beanbag in relief.

We have a great time. Lissa is really nice. She lets me try on her gear and we do each other's hair and paint each other's nails. I mean, I know I said I wasn't interested in cosmetics, but we're only talking nails here, and I know I said I always scrape my hair back out of the way in a ponytail, but that was some time ago. I've grown up a bit since then and it's good to try something new.

Lissa goes first and paints stripes on my nails, not very professionally, though I don't tell her that, but then I'm spoiled; I've only ever had Nikki do them before. When it's my turn, I paint tiny little stars on hers in different colours.

'Where did you learn to do that?' she gasps. 'They're gorgeous!'

'My sister taught me,' I say, pleased with her reaction. I'm surprised how much I'm enjoying myself. This is not the sort of stuff I'd normally get up to with Austen.

'I wish I had a sister like yours,' she says and I think to myself, *No, you don't*. But then I feel sad and bad at the same time. Because the truth is, I realize, Nikki can be a bit of a nightmare, but in other ways she is a pretty good big sister.

All of a sudden I have an overwhelming urge

to tell Lissa all about her. Funny that, because when I started at Riverside Academy, she was the last person I would've wanted to find out about Nikki. I was wary of Lissa at first, I think a lot of people were. I thought she was a snob. But she's not, she's just posh which is a different thing. Her accent makes her sound like she knows it all, but she doesn't. It's not her fault she talks like that.

But now I think she might understand.

She understood how I felt when Tash was picked for netball instead of me.

She's the only one of the Gang of Four who wants to see me at weekends.

And we're on the School Council together.

I take a deep breath. 'Have you got any sparkly polish?' I ask. Because I've made up my mind. I'm going to finish off her nails and at the same time, I'll tell her all about Nikki. That way I won't have to look at her while I'm explaining.

'In the drawer behind you,' she says, admiring her nails.

I turn round to open it. Life is strange. I always thought it would be Tash I'd confess my secret to first.

But then I snatch my hand back as if it's been

burned. Because Lissa yells, 'NOT THAT ONE, STUPID! THE ONE UNDERNEATH!'

I stare at her in shock.

'Sorry!' she says, her face bright red. 'Private stuff in there. You know.'

No, I don't know. I suppose she's started her periods, unlike me, and doesn't want me to know. But there's no need to screech at me like that. It's perfectly natural and I have seen the tampons and towels Nikki and my mum use; it's no big deal.

I sit there wondering what to say, but then there's a knock at the door and Mrs Hamilton enters with a tray of sandwiches. 'Time for your snack,' she says brightly.

Lissa rolls her eyes. What is wrong with her today?

'Thank you,' I say, feeling a bit awkward as she places the tray on the bedside table. 'They look nice,' I add, just to be polite and to make up for Lissa's distinct lack of enthusiasm.

Mrs Hamilton smiles at me. 'Thank you, dear. Don't forget to eat them up, Melissa.'

Don't I get any? But when her mum leaves the room, Lissa shoves the plate towards me. 'Help yourself.'

I inspect them critically – cheese and spinach

in seedy bread. Nice enough, but not the sort of treat most mums serve up when your friends come round.

'Is your mum very health-conscious?' I ask.

Lissa scowls. 'She does my head in. She treats me like a kid.'

I take one to be polite, but Lissa ignores them. I don't think she's into healthy eating herself, even though her packed lunch every day is an advert for it. We tease her about it and then she nicks biscuits and chocolates from ours to get her own back.

Maybe that's what she's got hidden in that stupid drawer! A stash of chocolate bars!

I finish off her nails for her, but I don't tell her my secret after all. I don't want to any more, she's too moody.

A little bit later, Mrs Hamilton comes back up to fetch the tray. She frowns when she sees we've hardly touched the sandwiches.

'Have another one, Melissa,' she says, but Lissa says, 'No thanks.'

'Please!' Mrs Hamilton wafts the plate under her daughter's nose. 'Just a little one,' she says in a high, wheedling voice, like Lissa's still a baby and she's trying to coax her to eat.

Lissa stares up at her with cold eyes. 'Which part of *No thanks* don't you understand?' she says and thrusts the plate away from her.

That is so rude! I would never be that rude to my mum, especially in front of my friends.

But then my mum's not as annoying as Lissa's mother.

When she's gone I find myself wondering what is going on. Why is Lissa in such a foul mood? And why does her mother baby her so much? I mean, I don't agree with wasting food myself, there's too much waste of resources on our planet, but we didn't ask for those sandwiches and someone could always eat them up later. And, I hate to say this, but it's not as if they can't afford it.

But Lissa's mum acted like her daughter would drop down dead if she didn't eat.

OMG!

Lissa looks up to see me staring at her.

'What?'

'Are you anorexic?' I blurt out.

Even as I say it I know she can't be. Like I said, at school she's forever scoffing treats from our lunchboxes.

'No!'

To my relief she laughs out loud and I'm sure she's telling the truth. But then a funny thing happens. Her eyes fill up.

'Are you all right?' I say in alarm. Honestly, I don't know what to expect from her next. First she yells at me, then she's rude to her mum, now she's on the verge of tears.

She nods, scrubbing her eyes angrily with the palms of her hands. 'I'm fine. It's just . . .'

She hesitates, like she's about to tell me something important. But then her mother's voice comes floating up the stairs. 'Alice, dear? Would you like a lift home?'

Lissa growls deep in her throat with frustration as I scramble obediently to my feet.

'Better go,' I say to her. Then I call down to her mum, 'No thanks. I'll get the bus.'

'Afraid she'll come to face to face with your dad?' taunts Lissa.

'Yes, if you must know!' I admit and at last she gives me a watery smile.

'We need to keep those two well away from each other,' she says and I smile back and say, 'You bet!'

But I don't tell her I want to keep her mum well away from Nikki too.

She stands up and gives me a hug. 'I'm sorry, Ali, about . . . you know . . .'

'That's OK,' I say, though I haven't a clue what *you know* is.

I can't wait to get home.

I nearly told Lissa my secret.

And I have a funny feeling she nearly told me one too.

Chapter 21

Nikki and Greg have moved in together in their flash new apartment. Dad's not very happy. Actually, that's an understatement.

He and Nikki had a huge argument about it and said loads of very rude and unprintable things to each other. In the end he yelled, 'If you move in with that flaming tree-trunk, I'll never speak to you again!' and she yelled back, 'I can't think of a better flaming reason to move in with him then! I'm off!' and since then they haven't spoken.

On Sunday afternoon Mum and I go over to have a nose round the flat. Dad declined to join us.

'Why have you got these?' I ask, inspecting the brand-new pots and pans in Nikki's brand-new kitchen as she proudly plugs in her brand-new cappuccino machine. 'You can't cook.'

'They're Greg's. He thinks he's Jamie Oliver. Look.' She points to a row of cookery books on the shelf. One of them is called *From the Garden to the Table*; the one next to it, *Grow Your Dinner, Lose Your Food Miles*. I'm impressed.

'Stay for dinner if you want,' comes a voice from the next room where Greg's stretched out in front of their massive TV screen.

'Can we?' I ask, but Mum shakes her head and shouts back, 'No thanks, Greg love, I've got a joint of beef in the oven at home.'

Mum called him 'love'. Good sign. Now we've just got to get Dad to accept him.

'What's Dad got against Greg?' I ask quietly, so he can't hear.

Nikki snorts. Dad does that.

'Is it just because he plays for the Wanderers?'

'Yeah. And the rest.'

'Like?' I'm distracted by a nifty little saucepan with two little containers inside it. 'What's this for?'

'I dunno. Ask Greg.'

Greg appears at the door. 'It's a steamer. You must've seen one before. It cooks all your veg in one pan. Saves on fuel.'

'Cool. Can we get a steamer, Mum?'

'I think we can afford to heat a few rings on the cooker,' says Mum drily.

'That's not the point,' says Greg, then he stops as Mum gives him one of her looks. I'm not so easily intimidated.

'Burning fossil fuels,' I remind her, 'is damaging our planet.'

'You're a pair of fossils, you and Greg,' grumbles Mum, but she picks up the steamer and examines it. 'They've been around for years, these, but I've never used one. Do they work?' She and Greg start an in-depth discussion about steamers and I turn to watch Nikki battling with the cappuccino machine. I never realized it was so hard to make a cup of coffee.

'What is wrong with this stupid thing?' she says and bashes it hard. 'It should be getting warm or making some sort of noise.'

A domestic goddess my sister is not. 'So,' I say discreetly, 'while he's otherwise engaged, tell me what else Dad's got against Greg.'

'Huh!' she says, pushing her hair out of her eyes. 'Where do I begin?' She holds up her hand and starts ticking off a list on her fingers. Dad does that too.

'Number one. The fact that Greg earns in a month what Dad earns in a year.

'Number two. The fact that Greg drives a bigger, faster car than him. Actually, the fact that he drives a car in the first place instead of a van.'

Her voice gets louder as she warms to her subject.

'Number three. The fact that Greg, like me, actually enjoys what he does for a living.

'Number four. The fact that Greg knows how to give a girl a good time.

'Number five. The fact that Greg's family comes from Trinidad . . .'

'That is not true!' interrupts Mum, in the quiet but firm way she puts Dad straight when he's going off on one. 'Your father is many things, but he is not racist.'

Nikki looks shame-faced like Dad does when he knows he's been caught out. Greg looks amused. 'No, you're right, he's not,' my sister admits. 'Scratch that.' Then she spoils it by adding, 'But there's plenty more!

'Number five. The fact that Greg is twenty-two and can buy his own place and Dad's forty-four and still renting off the council.'

'Forty-five,' corrects Mum.

'Dad says it's better to rent than to buy in the present economic climate,' I point out, but she's not listening.

'Number six. The fact that Greg drinks champagne instead of real ale.

'Number seven –'

'You're scraping the barrel now, Nik. I'm quite partial to a pint of real ale myself. And I bet your dad's downed the odd glass of bubbly in his time.'

Greg doesn't look cross that his girlfriend is listing the reasons her father hates him. I think he's heard it all before. Nikki ignores him, just like Dad ignores everyone when he's on a roll.

'Number seven. The fact that Greg wears designer clothes.'

'Not all the time,' says Greg who's wearing a Belstaff vintage cafe racer T-shirt and Armani jeans for a lazy Sunday afternoon at home. (Trust me. I'm Nikki's sister. I know my designers.)

'Believe me, my father's version of cool is an old sweatshirt and a pair of tracky pants.

'Number eight –'

'He's not that bad,' interrupts Mum, looking indignant. 'In fact, he scrubs up quite well.'

Nikki's allegations are becoming wilder, just like Dad's when he's getting worked up.

'Number eight. The fact that Greg drinks cappuccino instead of builders' tea with two sugars.'

'Not in this place, I don't. You're supposed to switch it on first, Nik.' He flicks the switch at the socket and the machine immediately starts whirring and rattling.

'Number nine.' Nikki carries on regardless. 'He's never liked anyone I've ever been out with . . .

'Number ten –'

'At last, you're making sense,' says Mum.

'Really?' Nikki stops in surprise.

'Well, I think you've hit the nail on the head for once. It's not you her father objects to, Greg,' says Mum. 'It's anyone. It's hard for fathers when their little girls grow up.'

Especially if they grow up like Nikki.

'You're not the problem, Greg,' I explain kindly. 'It's Nikki.'

Greg lets out a belly laugh, which he immediately changes into a coughing fit. Nikki glares at me, her hand on her hip.

'What do you mean?'

'You're just like Dad.'

Nikki's eyes look like they are going to pop out of her head. The resemblance to Dad is scary.

'WHAT?' she yells in outrage. 'That *bad*-tempered, *loud*, opinionated, cantankerous, KNOW-IT-ALL, who's *always* got to be right and is never, *ever* wrong and who goes *on* and *on* and *on* and *on*, *all* the time and who's *always* got to have the last word . . .' She pauses for a quick intake of breath and gulps, 'He's a right drama queen. What *ever* makes you think I'm like him?'

'I have absolutely no idea,' says Greg, solemnly shaking his head, and Mum and I burst out laughing.

Nikki stares at us all in turn.

'What?' she says blankly. 'What's so funny?'

That night, at home after dinner, we clear the table then Mum and Dad sit down by the fire with the Sunday paper while I get on with my French homework. It's kind of the pattern for Sunday evenings at our house. A strange thing always happens to my parents when they settle down like this, full of roast dinner. They talk as if I'm not there. Lost behind their different sections of the paper, Mum with the News Review and a glass of wine, Dad with the sports pages and a pint of real ale, they forget that I am.

'Our Nikki's new flat is nice,' says Mum.

Grunt.

'You should go and see it.'

Snort.

'You've got to admit, whether you like it or not, she's done well for herself.'

Silence. Then, 'I know she has,' says Dad grudgingly.

Mum seizes her advantage. 'That Greg is quite a nice lad, Colin, when you get to know him. You'd be surprised.'

Sniff. 'No point in getting to know him is there?'

'What do you mean?'

'He won't be around for long. He'll get the boot soon enough, like all the rest. Then she'll come crawling back. You know what our Nikki's like.'

Surprisingly, Dad's voice sounds almost proud of what our Nikki's like. I hope he's wrong. I mean, I never thought I'd say it, but I miss Nikki. Home's not the same without her around. But I like Greg. I really do.

Dad takes a slurp of his beer, then another

one, and gives a quiet belch of satisfaction. 'Pardon me,' he says comfortably, setting his glass down. Then he turns the page of the paper and says expansively, 'Yes, she's one on her own, our Nikki. You could write a book about what she gets up to.'

There it is again. A definite note of pride in his voice. That beer must be good.

'A chip off the old block, if you ask me,' says Mum.

Dad chuckles. 'Not like our Alice.'

'Not a bit like our Alice.'

'Chalk and cheese.'

Silence. I wait. Go on, parents. It's my turn. Say something nice about me now.

'She's settled in all right at that new school,' says Mum, true to form.

'Aye, she has,' says Dad.

'Doing well in all her subjects.'

'Aye.'

'And she's got on that school-council thingy.'

'Didn't have them in my day.'

Silence. Is that it?

Alice goes to school.

Alice comes home again.

Couldn't write a bestseller about that, could

you? I wait for them to say something else but after a while my dad starts snoring.

I sigh deeply. My parents have got nothing more to say about me.

Even they think I'm boring.

Chapter 22

The hockey team's next game was at home, after school, so I stayed behind to watch. It was pouring with rain and the pitch was a total mudbath. But they won, three—nil, even though they were slipping everywhere! Dani scored two goals and Lissa scored one. Dani was phenomenal. Mrs Waters says in all the years she's been playing, she's never seen anyone like her, and she's going to go far. She's put her in for a county trial after half term, lucky thing.

By the end of the game, you couldn't tell one person from the other, they were all plastered in mud from head to foot. But it was worth it, to be cheered and clapped off the field like that.

Mrs Hamilton was there under a massive umbrella and when she saw me getting wet she made me stand under it with her. She never stopped complaining about the state of the pitch and she kept calling out in her posh, high voice every time Lissa came anywhere near the ball.

But at least Lissa's mum was there. Dani and Tash had nobody watching them except me. They didn't seem to mind though. I guess their mums are single parents so they're out working. I know Dani's mum is a nurse, but I don't know what Tash's mum does for a living.

I'd have given anything to be on that pitch playing with them, mudbath or not. Still, I'm on the School Council and that's a full-time job in itself, let me tell you.

It's going really well. We've had our first meeting and it had an agenda, which was circulated to all the members beforehand. It had three items on it.

1. Address and welcome to the new members of the School Council by the headmistress.
2. An outline of the aims and objectives of the School Council.
3. Fundraising.

'Thrillsville!' drawled Tash when she saw the agenda and she yawned out loud, patting her mouth with her palm. Dani laughed. I couldn't blame them, it didn't sound exactly mind-blowing. But actually the meeting was better than I thought it would be.

It was item three that was the interesting one. Mrs Shepherd said that after the wet start to the new season, she would like to build a new all-weather pitch for hockey, which made Lissa and me sit up. But then she explained that funding had been cut and we groaned.

'So, we're going to have to raise the money ourselves,' she continued and we cheered up again. 'I intend to hold two fundraising events this term, one before half term for the Lower School and one at Christmas for the Upper School. I will need two Lower School students and two Upper School students to take charge of setting these up.'

A forest of hands shot up and, guess what? Lissa and I were chosen to organize the Lower School fundraising evening!

The next day we tell everyone in our form about it and ask them for their ideas.

'Let's have a disco!' says Tash and everyone cheers.

'What about an auction?' says Chantelle. 'They

did one at my dad's work for charity and they made loads.'

'An auction?' repeats Zadie, looking a bit sneery, which actually I think is her default expression.

'Don't laugh! It was a special kind of auction called an auction of promises where people promise to do things for you and you bid for them.'

'Like what? Maths homework? I'd pay someone to do that for me!' says Dani, quick as a flash, and everybody laughs.

'If you like. It could be anything. I'll ask my mum to put up a prize for someone to get their nails done at the salon she goes to.'

'My auntie works in Cuts and Colours. She'll cut your hair for you if you want!' says Georgia and then everyone starts competing to offer the services of mums and dads and aunties and uncles.

'You could donate things too,' says Georgia. 'I've got a signed photo of Titch Mooney you can have!'

Dani's mouth drops open. Titch Mooney is her footballing hero.

'Don't you want it?' she asks Georgia.

'I've got two the same.'

'OMG! That's mine! Don't anyone else bid for it!' gasps Dani, and she sounds almost girly.

'I'd rather have a photo of his girlfriend!' says Tash and everyone starts discussing the merits of the golden pair at the tops of their voices because, of course, Titch Mooney just happens to be Alana de Silva's latest. 'An evening with Alana de Silva!' Tash rolls her eyes. 'Now that's what I'd call a prize worth winning. I'm going to write to her on her website and ask her if she'll put herself up for a prize.'

'She'd never do that!' scoffs Dani, but Tash insists it's worth a try.

'It looks like an auction of promises is a popular choice,' says Miss Webb. 'But does anyone have any more ideas?'

'My neighbour walked the Great Wall of China to raise money for the hospice,' says Chloe.

'Too far,' says Miss Webb.

'Someone in the paper climbed Everest,' says Emma, not to be outdone.

'Too high,' says Miss Webb.

'We could cycle from John o' Groats to Land's End,' suggests Tori. 'I've never been to Scotland.'

'I have,' says Dani. 'It's really hilly.'

'And I haven't got a bike,' Tash points out.

'Think of something closer to home,' says Miss Webb. 'Any more suggestions?'

There are loads. Mostly along the lines of skydiving, parachute jumping, hang gliding, bungee jumping and every other extreme sport you can think of.

'I was thinking of something a little safer,' says Miss Webb, her hands over her ears as people yell out their suggestions. 'And quieter. How about a sponsored silence?'

'NOOOOOOOO!!!!!!!' everyone shouts but then someone suggests a school sleepover and everyone shouts, 'YEEEEEESSSSSS!!!!' except for Miss Webb who pulls a face.

Then I have an idea. Something Austen was telling me they had at his school. 'What about a peace garden?'

'What's a peace garden?' Thirty faces, including the teacher's, are staring at me.

'Um, well, they started off as memorials to people who had died in wars . . .'

'A war memorial?' Even Lissa looks confused.

'No, they don't have to be that. They're just gardens . . . We could create one here at school.'

'What for?'

'They're peaceful. They've got flowers and

fountains and things. You go and sit in it if you want to be quiet.'

I wish people weren't staring at me as if I had grown another head or something.

'That's a lovely idea, Alice,' says Miss Webb, who is obviously the only person who thinks it is. 'But how would it raise money?'

'Um . . .' I hadn't thought of that. 'I suppose you could charge people to go in.'

'Pay to go and sit in an old garden and be quiet?' says Chantelle.

'It's supposed to be fun,' says Georgia.

'I'd rather go paintballing,' says Dani.

'YEEEEEESSSSSS!!!!!' People start cheering and whooping and banging the desks. The door opens. Mrs Shepherd is standing there. Everyone falls silent.

'Ideas for fundraising!' explains Miss Webb, looking embarrassed like it was *her* that was making all the noise. The headmistress raises one eyebrow in query.

'Paintballing!' confesses Miss Webb.

'*Paint*balling?' repeats the head, as though we wanted to stab teachers or eat polar bears. 'Mmm. Not exactly what I had in mind.'

She peers over her spectacles and makes a

sweeping search of the room, her eyes coming to rest on me. My stomach lurches. It's not fair. I was the only one *not* making a noise!

'Alice,' she says. 'Tomorrow lunchtime I would like you to bring me some *sensible* ideas for raising money.' And then she disappears off down the corridor.

'Alice is full of sensible ideas,' Georgia says, but it doesn't sound like a compliment.

'Like a peace garden,' says Zadie.

'Bor-ing!' says Chantelle and a titter runs through the class. My cheeks grow warm.

'I think it's a great idea, Ali,' declares Tash, glaring at everyone. But I know she's lying.

I don't want a peace garden any more.

'A garden would take a long time to establish,' says Miss Webb. 'What we need is a one-off event that will raise money quickly.'

It looks like a straight choice between a disco or an auction or a sleepover.

Unless I can come up with something different.

Chapter 23

That night I tell my parents all about our Great Fundraising Venture. Of course, my dad has a grumble, saying things like, 'A school like that, you'd think they could afford to buy their own all-weather pitch,' and, 'Expecting us to fork out all the time.' But then, when Mum starts suggesting things, he gets into it too and once they get going the pair of them are worse than my classmates, trying to outdo each other.

'A cake sale,' says Mum. 'Or a cheese-and-wine evening.'

'Washing cars,' says Dad.

'Bor-ing!' I say and then wish I hadn't because immediately it reminds me of Chantelle.

'A Christmas bazaar.'

'A summer fete.'

'It's October!' I point out.

'A teddy-bears' picnic.'

'How old do you think we are?'

'Bingo.'

'I said, *How old do you think we are?*' But they're not listening.

'Snail-racing.'

'Ferret-racing . . .'

I need to talk to someone sensible. Not Austen! Not after the peace garden bombed so badly. So I ring Lissa instead, but she's not having much luck either. Her parents have just come up with corporate fundraising ideas, which basically means you ask someone rich to sponsor you.

'Well, maybe that's not such a bad idea,' I say, thinking about it. 'You must know loads of rich people.'

'Yeah, we do, but they're all tight. Anyway, we're supposed to organize an event, Miss Webb says, not just ask people for money.'

She's right. I hang up. Peals of laughter come from the lounge where my forty-odd-year-old parents are having the time of their lives vying with each other to think of the silliest fundraising activity.

'Welly wanging!' shouts my dad.

'Splat-the-rat!' squeals my mum.

They really do need to get a life.

I sigh deeply. This is way, way harder than I thought it would be. And I need desperately to come up with something good that everyone will like. It's really important to me.

Because, deep down, I'm afraid I've done something stupid. I've been so intent on proving to the world – and myself – that I'm nothing like my sister, I've gone too much the other way. I've forced myself into a corner. Now everyone thinks I'm something I'm not.

Everyone thinks I'm boring.

So now I want more than anything to prove to everyone that actually ALICE GRIMES IS NOT BORING. Just because I'm not amazing at sport like Dani or beautiful and funny like Tash or posh and driven like Lissa or celeb-mad like the Barbies, it doesn't mean I'm a loser. Yes, I happen to have a social conscience. But I want to have fun, like everyone else, I really do!

There's really only one person who can help me get out of this fix.

Nikki.

I ring her. And amazingly get straight through. 'Where are you?' I can hear loud music, cheering, a voice on a microphone, laughter, applause. The sound of people having a good time.

'Fashion show. What do you want?'

'Nothing.'

'I'm busy, Alice!'

I don't know what to say. Tears prick my eyes. I shouldn't have rung her.

'What's up, Ali?' Her voice is impatient. 'What is it?'

'I need help.' My voice is little more than a whisper.

'Why? What's happened?'

'Nothing! It's just school.'

'People being mean to you?' My sister's voice is gentler now. It makes the tears spill and my nose run.

'No,' I say, but it comes out all croaky. I clear my throat. 'I need some help with the School Council.'

'You're asking me for help with *schoolwork*?' She sounds incredulous. 'Ask Mum or Dad.'

'I need somebody *sensible*.'

Pause. Then her voice comes back, pleased this time. 'What is it? Make it quick.'

'I need to think of a one-off fundraising event

that will be a lot of fun and will make a lot of money.'

Silence. I can almost hear the pinging of ideas bouncing off her brain. Then she says, 'Get yourself over here. Now.'

'Where?'

'City Hall.'

'How?'

'I'm calling you a taxi. Don't tell Dad! He'll say no.'

And before I have time to object she hangs up.

I feel a stir of excitement in my stomach. Alice sneaking out at night without her parents knowing! Whatever next? I don't feel like me; I feel like my sister.

I wish Georgia and Zadie and Chantelle and all those other girls in my class who think I'm boring could see me now.

I haven't got much time to lose; the taxi will be here soon. I make sure I've got my key on me, then open the door to the lounge.

My parents have had so much fun they've collapsed with exhaustion and are sprawled on the sofa together listening to dreadful eighties music from their youth.

'I'm going to bed,' I inform them icily, 'and I don't want to be disturbed!'

'Sorry,' says Mum meekly. 'We got carried away.'

'Well, just make sure you keep the noise down,' I say sternly and close the door. Then I put my ear to it. My parents are sniggering away to themselves like a pair of naughty kids. Well done, Alice.

I let myself silently out of the back door and wait for the taxi. When it appears I say, 'City Hall,' with as much authority as I can muster. Ten minutes later, the taxi draws up outside the big grey building with the stone columns in the centre of town.

'Blimey!' says the taxi driver, 'Get an eyeful of that!'

My sister is waiting on the steps for me. She's covered from head to toe in gold paint and is dressed in a black corset and silk knickers and a diamanté eye-mask. Her hair is piled up on her head with a plume of feathers on top.

Dad would have a fit!

The taxi driver jumps out on the pretence of opening my door but I know it's because he wants a better look.

'You must be freezing!' I say to her but she ignores me and thrusts some notes into his hand. He can't take his eyes off her. 'Come on,' she says, ignoring him in turn, and takes me by the arm.

Inside, the huge public room of the hall where they hold the spring show and the panto and meetings about council cuts has been transformed. Rows and rows of seats filled with excited, chattering women are facing a long catwalk, which leads off the stage, and there are lights and flowers everywhere. The place is packed.

I stand at the back. Then I freeze. My eyes are drawn to a woman sitting a few rows in front of me. She's got carefully set hair and she's wearing a silk scarf and, even though I can only see her back view, I'd recognize her anywhere.

It's Mrs Hamilton.

I feel myself starting to panic. If she sees me here she'll tell Lissa. Then Lissa will ask me about it in front of the others and someone will put two and two together and my secret will be out.

'Stay here,' says Nikki, oblivious to it all. 'It's nearly over. Just the finale to go.' And she disappears.

And then I nearly jump out of my skin as music

blasts and smoke swirls across the stage and tall, skinny, long-legged girls wearing a whole spectrum of totally crazy outfits and impossibly high heels stride down the catwalk in front of me. Everyone bursts into applause.

They charge up and down for a while with blank expressions, twirling and prancing and sweeping past each other like cars on a Formula One track. Goodness knows how they don't collide. People start clapping in rhythm and for a moment it becomes quite jolly. Then suddenly there is a total explosion of light and sound as fireworks ignite and lights start dipping and swirling and the music pulses so loud it threatens to burst your eardrums, and my sister appears on a platform that shoots sparks right up to the ceiling, held high by four toned, bronzed, bare-chested guys.

And the whole room erupts. Including Mrs Hamilton.

She's always been an exhibitionist, our Nik.

Chapter 24

After the show is over, Nikki throws a coat over her costume and we get into a taxi. I glance around nervously but there's no sign of Mrs Hamilton.

'Where we going?'

'Back to mine. Can't really go out on the town dressed like this.' She glances at her watch. 'Don't worry, Cinders. I'll make sure you're home before you turn into a pumpkin.'

'Cinderella didn't turn into a pumpkin. Her coach did,' I point out and she yawns and says, 'Alice! Who cares?'

But then she listens to me as I tell her how people laughed at me at school for being boring.

Greg doesn't bat an eyelid when I turn up with Nik. He doesn't seem in the least bit surprised either that his girlfriend has changed colour and is dressed like a bunny girl. He just fetches another plate and divides the spaghetti carbonara between three while she jumps in the shower.

Scrubbed clean and sat at the table in her pyjamas, Nikki looks totally different now. She looks like my sister again, young and pretty.

'No wine with the meal?' she says, eyeing her glass of Perrier water with disappointment.

'Too late,' says Greg. 'You've got work in the morning.' If Dad had said that to her she'd have thrown a wobbly, but she just pulls a face and swigs back her water.

'What did you think of it then?' she asks me, forking pasta into her mouth.

'What?'

'The fashion show, idiot.'

'It was OK.'

Nikki rolls her eyes and stares out of the window.

I don't blame her. I sound really grudging. But from me this is praise indeed. I don't approve of fashion, she knows that.

'Why did you ask me to come?' I ask.

'Why did you ask me for help?' she snaps, continuing to stare through the window at the city lights below, her chin on her hand. She's mad at me.

Nikki was good tonight. She was better than good; she was the star of the show. No one could take their eyes off her. She was the reason it all came together. She pulled the whole thing off, just like Dani does on the hockey pitch.

My sister is the Dani of the catwalk.

'Actually,' I whisper. 'I thought you were brilliant.'

'Halleluiah!' she shouts and flings her arms round me. Then she grabs me by the shoulders so hard it hurts and stares intently into my eyes.

'Listen to me, Alice.' Her voice is serious. 'I thought you needed a fundraising event?'

'I do.'

'One that would raise a lot of money.'

'I do.'

'One that is fun and exciting.'

'I do.'

'One that will make those snotty-nosed divas in that posh school of yours sit up and take notice of you.'

'I do.'

'You two getting married?' asks Greg and we laugh and the tension breaks between us as she lets me go at last.

'They're not snotty-nosed divas,' I say belatedly. 'They're my friends.'

'Then show your *friends* what you're made of. Impress them.'

'How?'

'Do a fashion show.'

'What?'

'You heard me.' Her face is alight. 'You've seen it, you've seen what they're like. They're amazing!'

'I know . . .'

'Come on, Alice, fashion rocks! Put on a fashion extravaganza like the one you saw tonight and show them all what you're really made of! Give Riverside Academy for Girls an all-out, crazy, singing and dancing night to remember – no holds barred.'

My skin tingles with excitement. They'd love it; I know they would! Tash, Lissa, Georgia, Zadie, Chantelle, all of them. (Maybe not Dani.) And it would show them once and for all that Alice Grimes wasn't the most boring person in the world.

'Where would I get the clothes from?'

'I've got contacts,' she says. 'I'll help you.'

'What about the music?'

'No problem.'

'And the catwalk and the lights and the flowers and . . .?'

'I told you – I'll give you a hand. *We'll* give you a hand . . . won't we, Greg?'

'Course we will.' Greg nods obligingly and the three of us grin at each other. Between us, anything is possible.

'I promise you, it will be sensational!' says Nikki, aglow. 'And not only will everyone have the night of their lives but you'll make loads and loads of money in the process. It's a no-brainer!'

My smile fades.

'I don't know . . .'

'What do you mean, you don't know?' Nikki looks at me as if I've taken leave of my senses. Perhaps I have.

'It's wrong,' I say blankly.

'What's wrong?'

'Fashion.'

Nikki makes a growling sound in her throat, like an angry dog. 'What? You mean the *whole* of the fashion industry is wrong?'

'Well . . .' I struggle to make sense of what I'm thinking. 'It's all about consumerism, isn't it?'

'Here we go!'

'No, listen! It's just a way of getting people to

spend money. On more clothes. Clothes they don't need and they can't afford . . .'

'. . . made by people who work long hours and get paid too little for it.'

I look up at Greg in surprise as he finishes off my thoughts. Is he mocking me?

Nikki glares at him. 'Don't you start!'

'It's true, Nik. Alice is right, you know she is.'

'Doesn't stop you buying your Armani jeans, does it?'

'No, but it doesn't make it right,' he says mildly.

'You're just a pair of old crusties . . .'

'I'm not a crusty!' I say, stung to the core, then I add quickly. 'Neither is Greg!'

Obviously Greg isn't. He's one of the coolest people I know. *The* coolest person I know. I try to explain my feelings to Nik because it's important, it really is.

'I like looking good, of course I do. But fashion exploits too many people. Especially in poor countries.'

'It exploits women in the West too. All those girls who aspire to be a size zero, like the skinny, human coat-hangers you see on the catwalk,' remarks Greg.

'What?' splutters Nikki, and I rush to Greg's defence.

'Like that girl in the paper who starved herself to death, remember?' A vision of Lissa swims into my head, saying no to her mum's sandwiches, but I push it away. Not now. I've got enough to deal with here.

Greg shakes his head. 'Be honest, Nik. It worries you too. You've said so yourself.'

Nikki exhales slowly. 'All right. I'm not saying it's perfect. I think that side of the industry is changing, I'm glad to say. We're not all size zero you know,' she adds.

'Thank goodness,' says Greg, only next to him she is. He gives her a hug and she practically disappears inside his arms. Everybody's tiny compared to him.

'But people still have too many clothes,' I persist. Then I add regretfully, 'I can't do it, Nikki. I can't promote an event that encourages people to spend more than they can afford on clothes they don't need just to raise money for an all-weather pitch.'

'You are so like Dad,' she mutters. 'So critical!'

But she's wrong. Dad doesn't know the first thing about fashion. He just hates the lifestyle she leads. He doesn't know she's changed since she moved in with Greg. She's calmed down a lot.

'I'm sorry, I really am.' I look from one to the other. 'I would love more than anything to go into school tomorrow and say, *Let's do a fashion show*, honest I would. But I can't help the way I feel.'

Greg nods understandingly, but Nikki looks really disappointed.

'You spend too much time with that nerdy, eco-warrior boyfriend of yours, that's your trouble. You just want to be *ethical*.' She says 'ethical' like it's an insult.

'No I don't. I hardly see Austen nowadays!'

It's true. Since I said I couldn't go to the cinema with him we've hardly spoken. I've been busy with my new friends and the School Council and I assumed he was busy too. It dawns on me that I've been so wrapped up in my new life, I've more or less forgotten about my old one.

I've been a flaky friend to Austen.

'Anyway, he's not my boyfriend,' I add out of habit, but she's not listening.

'It could have been great,' she continues. 'Shame. I was looking forward to getting involved.

Ah well, better get you home before the 'rents discover you've run away. I'll call you a cab.'

'It's all right, I can drive her,' says Greg.

'There's no need.'

'I insist,' he says, picking up his keys and giving them a little twirl. 'Come on, Alice. I've got something I want to talk to you about. We can chat on the way.'

'What?' asks Nikki. 'Is it about my birthday?' But Greg just taps the side of his nose and grins.

'Oooohh, secrets!' mocks Nikki. 'Don't worry, I'll get it out of you when you get back.'

'Look forward to it!' He grins, but she yawns and says, 'Nah, actually, I'm off to bed. I need an early night. Don't wake me up when you get home – I need my beauty sleep.'

Since when did our Nikki go in for early nights? OK, it is nearly midnight but, believe me, that's early for her. Dad would be pleased if he could see how much she's changed.

But he's not going to, is he? Because he's as pig-headed as she is.

Maybe I'm being pig-headed too.

When we get home, Greg wants to knock on the front door and deliver me back safely into my parents' arms but I manage to persuade him that is not a good plan.

'You Grimes Girls!' he says, shaking his head. 'I feel sorry for your old man.' But he does as he's told and drops me off at the end of the street and I manage to slip back into the house with no difficulty whatsoever. As I tiptoe upstairs I can hear Dad's loud and Mum's marginally quieter snores pulsating from their room. No wonder Nikki got away with sneaking in and out for years.

I get into bed and hug Greg's idea to me like a warm, fluffy cushion.

The idea he outlined to me on the way home in the car.

The idea that puts the *fun* back into *fun*draising.

The idea that will show everyone that Alice Grimes is definitely *not* the most boring person in the world once and for all.

I have to convince Lissa that she wants to do it too. But before I talk to her, I need to talk to someone else first. No time to lose.

Even though it's gone midnight, I ring Austen.

Chapter 25

Austen is brilliant. We talk for ages. He comes up with loads of ideas to add to Greg's, just like Greg said he would, even though he's never actually met him.

Then I ring Lissa and, even though it's now tomorrow, the first thing she says to me is, 'What were you doing at the fashion show tonight?'

Her mum had spotted me after all.

I fight down the panic and think quickly. 'My sister, er . . . wanted me to go with her.'

'Lucky! My mum said it was awesome. What did you think of ?'

'Listen!' I interrupt her in mid flow. 'I've got an idea for fundraising . . .' I outline the plan quickly and to my delight she's totally up for it.

Sorted. Now all I have to do tomorrow morning is convince the others.

*

'A fashion show?'

Everyone's eyes light up except for Dani's, which glaze over. As it's Dani, I don't take it personally.

'Will we all get a chance to be models?' asks Georgia.

'Yes.'

'OMG!' All Tash's dreams have come true. 'I get to go on the catwalk! There will be a catwalk, won't there?'

'Yes, there will be a catwalk.'

She gives a small scream and looks as if she's about to faint with pleasure. Everyone starts clamouring at once.

'Whose clothes will we be wearing?'

'New Look! I bet it's New Look.'

'Maybe it's Topshop? Can I wear Topshop?'

'No, we'll be wearing a new label.'

The decibels rise. Now it sounds like a swarm of bees have zoomed in through the classroom window and are frantically buzzing around.

'A new label!'

'What's it called?'

'FC.'

'FCUK?'

'No, just FC.'

'Never heard of it.'

'Do you mean FC as in French Connection?'

'No, I mean FC as in *Fashion with a Conscience*,' I say bravely. Austen's slogan.

The buzzing stops.

'Bor-ing!' says Georgia and my heart sinks.

But Lissa says, 'Shut up, Georgia and listen,' and Georgia is so surprised, she does as she's told for once.

Everyone is looking at me. Form period on Friday morning is almost over, time is running out. Just a few hours left to get this idea off the ground. I swallow hard. FC is a great idea.

But, first, I have to persuade my class.

And, second, I have to persuade Mrs Shepherd.

Deep breath. Here goes.

'*Fashion with a Conscience* means that we recycle our old clothes instead of buying new ones.'

'We parade around on the catwalk in our old clothes?' Ella sounds as if she can't believe her ears.

'Yep. The older the better.'

Dani perks up a bit. On the other hand, Tash doesn't seem quite so excited any more.

'In front of the whole school?' she says, looking perplexed. 'Do you mean in our favourite buys?'

'No. I'm talking about the stuff you've got hanging in the backs of your wardrobes that you never ever wear.'

People start whispering and giggling. I can feel myself going red.

'Things we don't like?' Tash is struggling hard to understand. 'Like impulse buys?'

'Yeah. And things you've forgotten all about. If you don't like it, change it.'

'Change it?'

'Adapt it. Turn it round. Glam it up. Make it now.'

Most people are staring at me blankly. But one or two are starting to look interested.

'Look in your attics,' I tell them.

'I don't put clothes in my attic,' says Zadie, sounding offended, and people start laughing out loud.

'No,' says Lissa, coming to my aid. 'But if your mum is anything like mine she does. Ask her to go through her old stuff.'

'Our loft could do with a good clear-out,' says Tash thoughtfully.

'My mum's got a load of posh frocks she doesn't wear any more because they're out of date,' explains Lissa. 'But she won't throw them away because they were so expensive. They're just festering away at the back of her wardrobe. Some of them are left over from the twentieth century.'

Everyone starts chipping in.

'My mum's still got some eighties gear somewhere. Stuff from when she was a teenager.'

'I love eighties gear! It's dead retro.'

'My mum wore this sort of jumpsuit thing to a party last week. She bought it about twenty years ago. Actually, she looked really cool.'

'My mum's still got a maxi-dress from the seventies!'

'The seventies! Your mum must be ancient!'

'She is.'

'I love maxi-dresses!'

'My gran's still got stuff from the sixties. Mary Quant dresses.'

'OMG! They're vintage, they are. I love vintage!'

'She should sell them on eBay. She'd make a fortune.'

'She's got bell-bottom jeans as well. With real bells! Levis.'

'Did they have them in those days? I've got Levis!'

'Me too!'

'Don't you love those tie-dye T-shirts they used to have in the sixties?'

'And those fitted dresses with the wide belts and huge skirts they used to have in the fifties?'

'Like the ones they wore in *Grease*?'

'Yeah. And in *Dirty Dancing*.'

Everyone is babbling away with excitement at the tops of their voices. Miss Webb catches my eye and smiles. She's on my side, I can tell.

'Do you want to do it then, 7LW?' she asks. 'Do you want to put on a Fashion Show with a Conscience to raise money for the new all-weather pitch?'

'YEEEEEEEESSSSSSSS!!!!!'

Miss Webb laughs. 'There's your answer. I think it's a great idea. Well done, Alice and Lissa.'

'Actually,' says Lissa modestly, 'it was Ali's idea.'

All eyes turn to me. I take a deep breath. If she can be honest, so can I.

'Actually,' I say, 'it was my sister's.'

'Cool sister,' says Georgia and smiles at me approvingly. I feel like I'm going to faint.

'Well, whoever's idea it was,' says Miss Webb, 'you've won us over.'

I hesitate. 'There's just one more thing . . .'

'What is it, Alice?'

166

'I don't think all the money we raise should go towards the all-weather pitch.'

Miss Webb raises her eyebrows. 'Why ever not?'

'I think we should split it between the all-weather pitch and supporting education in Somalia. We could adopt a school, help them buy books. You see, Miss, we can afford it; they can't.'

Everyone cheers and our form teacher smiles approvingly. 'I agree, Alice. But the problem is will Mrs Shepherd?'

Lissa, whose dad knows all about these things, pipes up, 'She will if it's pitched to her properly.'

'We could do a presentation,' suggests Dani.

'Like on *The Apprentice*!' squeals Tash. 'I wanna be on Ali's team!'

'So do I!' shout Lissa and Dani, and soon everyone else is clamouring to be on my team too. But then the bell goes and everyone groans as Miss Webb says, 'There's no time left. Alice, it's all down to you!'

She asks me to stay behind for a quick discussion. That's when, with no one else listening, I outline my whole plan to her, telling her exactly what I've got in mind. And then she squeals too, just like Tash, and bounces up and down with delight.

'But remember, Alice,' she warns me, once she's calmed down, 'Riverside Academy has never done anything like this before. You'll have your work cut out to persuade the head a fashion show is a good idea. Tell her how much you expect an event like this to raise. But keep it short and *don't* go into too much detail. You know what I mean.'

I nod fervently. 'Don't worry, Miss Webb.' But then I feel nervous. 'Tash is right, you know. I feel a bit like I'm on *The Apprentice*.'

She smiles understandingly. 'And Mrs Shepherd is Lord Sugar!' Then she glances guiltily at the classroom door as if she's half-expecting the headmistress to be lurking there, earwigging. I think she's afraid she'll come in and tell her she's fired.

Maybe she will after the show!

At lunchtime I sit outside Mrs Shepherd's office on my own, watching the hands of the clock move. It's so quiet I can hear my stomach churning. A low buzz of noise can be heard from the dining hall, as well as odd shrieks from the distant playing fields, but this part of the school, normally out of bounds to pupils, is quiet and deserted. As the minutes tick by, all my confidence drains away and I start to remember how I felt that very first morning sitting in the Great Hall, dreading the moment the head would appear. Scared. Alone. Sick to my stomach.

I was wrong. I can't do this by myself.

Suddenly my eye is caught by a movement at the end of the corridor. Something has appeared from behind the corner out of nowhere. A girl's face is grinning manically at me. Not a real face. It's a drawing, stuck on to the end of a ruler, a sketch of someone with long fair hair and distinctive ornate clips. The word **GO** is written beneath it in bold black letters. Clutching it is a blazer-clad arm.

What is going on?

Another one appears, right below it, only this time it's got a cheeky freckly face and spiky hair, with the word **TEAM** written beneath it. Then a third one pops up, a brown smiley face with black hair threaded into blue and yellow beads bearing the name **ALI**. As the three faces jiggle about on their ruler bodies in a mad dance, I start to giggle. Then behind me a door opens and a voice calls, 'Come in, Alice!' and the three smiley heads vanish in a trice.

I stand up, take a deep breath and step inside

Mrs Shepherd's Inner Sanctum. I'm not alone or scared any more. How could I be, with Team Ali behind me? I do exactly what Miss Webb told me to and keep it short, and I definitely don't go into too much detail.

And it works.

She says yes!

Chapter 26

After that there's no time to lose and preparations for the fashion show are soon underway. Half term is looming. The first thing I want to do is get the Gang of Four and Austen together so I invite them all over to my house on Saturday. Dani immediately says she can't come and I'm not surprised – fashion is hardly her thing.

Though I can't help feeling, if we are the Gang of Four, she could make the effort.

Tash says she'll try to make it. Then on Saturday afternoon she rings at the last minute to say she can't come after all and, even though she sounds genuinely fed up about it, I feel really let down.

'Typical!' says Lissa and I hope she's not going to go all moody on me. But then Austen arrives and I introduce them to each other and soon

171

they're getting on together like a house on fire.

We go up to my room and Austen outlines his plan to us.

'Ethical stands,' he says. 'That's what we need to greet people when they first come in. It'll get them in the right mindset.'

'What do you mean?' asks Lissa.

'Stalls selling recycled things. Like old denim jeans cut down to shorts . . .'

'Brilliant!' says Lissa, her eyes shining. 'We could sell necklaces made out of buttons too. They're dead easy to make and they look fantastic.'

'Absolutely,' says Austen and soon they are busy batting ideas for stalls at each other like they're on Centre Court at Wimbledon. I might as well not be there.

In the end I leave them to it and go downstairs to get some drinks. But then Nikki turns up to pick up her post and so I seize the opportunity to pick her brain. With Dad watching the Rovers and Mum out shopping, I have her undivided attention.

She is amazing. So amazing I take notes.

'I had absolutely no idea just how much goes into creating a fashion show,' I admit, scribbling away like mad.

'Tell me about it!' Her voice is full of contempt. 'People think it's just a few airheads strutting their stuff on a catwalk. They don't think about music and staging and costume and make-up and seating. And then you have to consider things like *angle* and *narrative* and *ethos* and *performance* . . .'

I keep scribbling as Nikki continues to outline how to put on a fashion event using words I never even knew existed. Tash doesn't know what she's missing.

I have to say my sister really knows her stuff. My admiration for her grows by the minute. I mean, I've always thought beneath it all Nikki is awesome in loads of ways, but I never knew quite how good she is at what she does. I wish Dad was here to see her so animated, so passionate, so professional . . . He should be proud of who she is, he should be shouting it from the rooftops.

So should I.

It's time I introduced her to my new friends. I should've done it ages ago.

'Come upstairs and meet Lissa,' I suggest, but she says, 'No, I can't, I've got to go. I'm working tonight.'

'Thanks for everything,' I say seriously. 'I won't let you down.'

Nikki's eyes grow warm and her arms enfold me in a soft, squishy, sweet-smelling hug. 'Course you won't, silly. Between you, me, Greg and old Earthy Penberthy up there, this fashion show is going to rock!'

In school on Monday we get down to business. What started off as a simple idea just grows and grows and grows. Everyone in the form pitches in: the Barbies, the Profs, Tash, who's in her element, even Dani who normally hates girly stuff.

Over the next week people raid their mums' wardrobes and their attics and the classroom begins to look like a jumble sale. So Miss Webb organizes some clothes rails and mirrors from the textiles department and Chantelle brings in loads of coat hangers because her mum works in a dry-cleaner's and we hang them all up. And now the classroom looks like a Next sale on Boxing Day.

Miss Webb is well pleased with us all. She says it's been a real bonding exercise.

And in the middle is me, directing operations!

I could never have done it on my own. But nobody here knows just how much Nikki has been behind the show. All the best ideas have come from her. Her and Greg.

Actually, Miss Webb knows. Because she's in on the secret.

The day before the show Mr McAdam, the caretaker, builds a catwalk for us leading off the stage all the way down the Great Hall and we spend the whole afternoon practising on it. Tash thinks she's in heaven. Afterwards I show Mr McAdam how I want the chairs set out and everyone helps.

'How come you know so much about fashion shows, Alice?' asks Georgia.

'I've been to one before.'

She looks at me with respect. 'Who with?'

'My sister.'

'Is she into fashion?' asks Zadie.

'Yes.' I take a deep breath. 'She's a model.'

'You never said!' Tash's head jerks up in surprise as Miss Webb gives me a warning look.

'What's her name?' asks Chantelle. Everyone is staring at me and I'm on the point of blurting it out, when Miss Webb answers, 'Nikki. Nikki Grimes.'

'Never heard of her!' says Zadie and everyone

laughs, except Tash who is looking hurt because I never told her my sister is a model.

I feel bad then. But the next minute the bell rings and Tash goes tearing off as per usual so I stop beating myself up about it.

She'll find out the truth soon enough.

Like everyone else.

Chapter 27

Tonight's the night!

We're on stage behind the curtains, all dressed in our gear and looking totally unrecognizable. I am soooo nervous. So is everyone else. The hall is full to bursting. All the tickets have been sold, but people are still turning up and asking for them at the door.

On the other side of the curtain, there is so much stuff going on in the Great Hall.

A big screen has been erected at the side of the stage where words flash on and off, pulsating in rhythm. Beneath it the rest of Year Seven, the warm-up act, clap and dance and chant in unison.

FC!
Fashion with a Conscience.
Fashion with a Mission.
Fashion for free!

FC!
Fashion with a Conscience.
Fashion with a vision.
Fashion for free!

FC!
Fashion with a Conscience.
Fashion on a budget.
Fashion for free!

FC!
Fashion with a Conscience.
Fashion for the future.
Fashion for free!

People laugh and take their seats, joining in the clapping. Soon they're chanting the words aloud from the screen and the hall vibrates with hundreds of voices.

'OMG!' squeals Dani, peeping between the curtains. 'Have you seen how many people are out there?'

'Leave that curtain alone, Danielle!' says Miss Webb and Dani drops it like a hot potato. But, when the teacher goes off to see to something, I can't resist taking a peek myself.

The Great Hall has been transformed. We all brought our largest pot plants from home to decorate the hall; no cut flowers allowed. Tash was worried because she didn't have any, but I gave her one of mine. Mrs Hamilton went out and bought a load specially, which was not really the idea, but I have to admit they do look good.

Nearly every seat is taken but there are still loads of people milling round the various stands manned by Year Eights and Nines who have helped us prepare for the big night.

One of the most popular is the Revamped Jewellery stall run by 8MF where unloved necklaces, bracelets and earrings have been dismantled to make sparkling new creations. Lissa's button necklaces are on display there too. Her mum made loads of them, apparently, and they're selling like hot cakes.

Another is the tie-dye area where old T-shirts have been reborn with bright splashes of colour and a demonstration is taking place by Austen who's had special permission to come in and help, being as most of the ideas for the stands came from him.

I hardly recognized him when he walked in. He's shaved his head and it really suits him and he was wearing a black-and-purple T-shirt of his own creation. Everyone immediately wanted to know who he was and I had to introduce him. Now, loads of girls are standing around, admiring his talents.

A demo is going on at Cut and Crop as well, where Year Nines are showing parents, siblings, grandparents and school governors how to turn an old pair of trousers into shorts or cropped trousers.

Next to that, Recyclebags is selling bags made out of sundresses, while across the way Skousers are doing a roaring trade in skirts made out of old jeans. At 8AP's Hot Legs stand, people are buying up legwarmers made from tights and socks as if there is no tomorrow.

Even the science department has come up trumps with shampoos to make your hair shine made from lemon and vinegar, face masks made from cucumber and egg white and soothing eye-pads made from tea bags!

I can see my mum and dad in the middle of the front row. Well done, Mum, for dragging Dad here.

'Come early,' was the last thing I'd said to them when I left the house this morning. 'Make sure you get a good seat.'

'What would I want to go to a flaming fashion show for?' I could hear Dad grumbling but Mum had said, 'Colin! You're going! End of!' so I knew she'd make sure he was there.

Nikki's coming too. And Greg. But not yet. They're not allowed to come till after the show starts.

I don't want anyone to see them.

'Is my mum here?' says Lissa in a low voice, and I peer around until I spot her elbowing her way past people to a spare seat. Oh no, it's right behind my parents. She sits down and smiles graciously at the people either side of her.

Mum turns round and Mrs Hamilton smiles graciously at her too.

Dad turns round and her smile freezes. I swallow hard.

'Yes. Second row from the front. Behind my dad.'

'Uh-oh.'

'Is mine here?' someone asks.

'Is mine?'

'Can you see if my gran's arrived yet?'

People start clamouring at me to look for their relations and Miss Webb says, 'Shush! Alice, come away from that curtain! We're about to start.'

The rappers finally come to a close and the last seats are grabbed and I stand there shaking with excitement, waiting to go on. As the lights go down, I feel a tug on my sleeve.

'Ali?'

'What?'

'Why didn't you tell me your sister was a model?' asks Tash.

'It's complicated!' I say and she looks crestfallen. But then I say, 'I'll tell you later, I promise,' and she brightens up.

'Alice Grimes, stop talking!' hisses Miss Webb, and my mouth clamps shut. As the music blasts out, she picks up the microphone and clears her throat. She's nervous too. She's our compere for the night.

'Break a leg, Miss!' I whisper.

'Break a leg, Alice!' she whispers back. Then she gives me a wink and steps through the gap in the curtain.

Chapter 28

One after the other we stride on to the catwalk through clouds of smoke and dry ice. Above the discordant, haunting music I can hear the audience gasp.

The theme is post-apocalyptic grunge – Greg's idea, choreographed by Nikki. We've messed up our planet and now we are down to the serious business of survival. It's bitterly cold and our clothes reflect that. We're all covered up in trousers, sweats, overcoats, boots, gloves, scarves, hats, hoods. Where heads are bare, hair is wild and messy. Faces are sallow. The look is bleak, grim, savage.

We turn, spread out, stop, pose, establish eye contact with the audience. You can sense them recoiling as we glare at them. This isn't what they expected.

I've trained the girls well, just as Nikki told me to. 'Work the audience,' she'd instructed, showing me how to do it. 'Make them feel your hate. They're responsible for destroying your planet.'

Our hostile eyes accuse them from blank, grey faces. *You did this to us. It's all your fault.* Miss Webb's voice rings out in a hollow monotone describing our world, but there's no need for words. I can tell from the shocked silence they understand.

Some of us go offstage to get changed while the rest parade up and down again, eyeballing the audience. I wriggle my way into a pair of cut-down jeans, an old white T-shirt with an orange one on top I've cut into a jagged fringe, and a blue-and-black bandanna I've made from a top I've grown out of. Then I zip Tash into a nude-coloured nineties evening dress of her mum's.

'This colour works brilliantly against your dark skin,' I say and she smiles.

'You really sound like you know what you're talking about, Ali.'

'I do, don't I?' I've surprised myself. I've learned a lot preparing for this show.

'Did you see their faces?' says Tash.

The angry, strident music comes to an abrupt stop and a soft, gentle harmony takes over.

Everyone pours off the stage and strips off their grunge to don outfits they have recycled themselves. From the other side of the curtains, I can hear Miss Webb's voice rising and falling.

'Consumerism, the rise in cheap clothing and poor practices in the fashion industry are all contributing to the destruction of our planet and unfortunately we are cooperating with it with our shopping habits.

'But it doesn't have to be like that. Our Lower School has taken on the challenge of ethical fashion and 7LW would like to present to you their own label, FC, made entirely from recycled clothing . . .'

'We're on!' I say to Tash and pull the curtain aside as we burst on to the catwalk.

'Alice is wearing an outfit she has put together herself from an old pair of jeans and a few old tops. With inventive use of the scissors and a needle and cotton, she has created this season's hottest look.'

Miss Webb pauses as I twirl and swirl in front of the audience who, uncertain at first, clap politely. But Austen whoops his appreciation and I smile with delight and everyone laughs and claps a bit harder.

'Tasheika has gone with the nineties look, bang on trend, and is wearing a dress of her mother's that she has salvaged from the loft and personalized herself. I think you would agree with me, she looks absolutely stunning. Thank you, Alice and Tasheika.'

We swish back down the catwalk, pivoting in a final turn before we disappear off stage and now we are applauded enthusiastically. Immediately we are replaced by Lissa and Dani.

'Another mum's dress comes out of the closet here,' begins Miss Webb. 'Lissa is looking sensational tonight in a figure-hugging black silk dress with padded shoulders that apparently belonged to *her* mother back in the eighties, which she's combined very successfully with a pair of Doc Martens.'

From the shocked expression on her mother's face I can tell she had absolutely no idea her daughter would be parading about in it tonight. Then someone in the audience says, 'Very nice!' and Mrs Hamilton beams proudly.

'Dani is wearing a pair of vintage Levis, a striped T-shirt and her father's black dinner jacket,' continues Miss Webb. Dani's short hair is sprayed into a quiff and Tash has painted long lashes above and below her right eye. 'The first and last time in my life I will ever wear make-up!' she'd protested, but the effect is striking.

I wish her dad could be here to see her in his dinner jacket. Her mum's here though and her sister. But there's no one here at all for Tash.

I haven't got time to think about that now. It's all going beautifully. One after the other every single member of 7LW appears on the catwalk to strut her stuff and the level of applause and cheering multiplies each time. Off stage we beam and hug each other in delight. Everyone – models, teachers, helpers, audience, is having a wonderful time.

But the best is yet to come.

Nobody knows about the next part of the evening except for Miss Webb and me.

Once everyone has done their bit, we all pile back on to the stage and everybody gets to their feet and applauds us. Then Miss Webb picks up the microphone again and asks the audience to sit back down in their seats and the performers to perch on the edge of the stage. Everyone in my class is laughing and chattering as we do as we're told. But my insides have turned to jelly.

'And now I have a surprise for you all,' says Miss

Webb when it's quiet once more. 'This evening we are joined by someone who knows both the glamour and the pitfalls of the fashion industry better than anyone. A young woman who is zooming to the top of her profession but who is herself concerned about its ethics. Someone who is proud to support FC. Ladies and gentlemen, this evening I am delighted to welcome to Riverside Academy the fantastic, the amazing . . .'

She pauses for effect.

'Who's she talking about?' says Tash.

'What's going on?' demands Lissa.

'Who is it?' asks Dani.

On the stage, excitement fizzes through my class as we sit in line like birds on a wire.

'. . . ALANA de SILVA!'

There is a moment of stunned silence. Tash's jaw has dropped open and her face is totally blank like her brain's been blown away. Then, to a fanfare of flashing lights and exploding fireworks and blasting music and tumultuous applause, the most infamous, influential, ingenious model of the moment strides on to the stage.

Alana de Silva.

Aka my sister.

Nikki Grimes.

Chapter 29

'What I don't understand is why you never told us your sister was Alana de Silva in the first place,' says Tash. 'If she was my sister I'd have shouted it from the rooftops.'

It's the morning after the fashion show and the Gang of Four have all met up for a coffee in town. It's the first time we've done this, all of us together, and it's such a cool thing to do. We've got so much to talk about we haven't stopped. But Tash's words make me go quiet.

'Were you ashamed of her?' asks Dani.

Tash shrieks. 'Dani! What a thing to say!'

But I try to answer honestly. 'Not ashamed! No!'

'Embarrassed?' she persists.

'No, of course not!' I rush to my own defence, but Dani looks sceptical. I'm not fooling anyone.

'No secrets, we said, remember?' Lissa reminds me.

I take a deep breath. I owe it to them. I owe it to my friends to be honest. I need to try and explain to them truthfully – and to myself – why I kept my sister's identity a secret.

'I'm not embarrassed by Nikki . . .'

'I should think not!' says Tash.

'. . . but I was a bit by Alana de Silva,' I admit.

'How could you? OMG! She's a star, she's the hottest thing on the planet, she's so talented, she's . . .'

'Shut up, Tash, and let her explain,' says Lissa.

'I know she's good at what she does. Though I never understood until recently just how good she is. And I'm proud of her, of course I am. But the fashion industry . . . I don't agree with it, you know what I'm like. All that waste. All that exploitation . . .' My voice tails off.

'It's more than that though, isn't it?' prompts Lissa and I nod.

Who would've thought Lissa could be so understanding? I guess we've got to know each other planning this show. And, even though I kept the surprise ending from her, she hasn't held it against me. Everyone waits patiently as I struggle to go on.

'She was always in the news for the wrong reasons. Like falling down drunk or getting into fights. And Nik's not really like that. My dad hates all that celebrity stuff . . .'

Though since last night, I'm not so sure. I saw the look on his face as she worked that catwalk. No one could've looked prouder than he did as Nikki took the event by storm. I think he saw for the first time what a true professional she was.

'And I did too,' I say, laying bare my soul for my friends' inspection. 'You see, that's not really her, that Bad Girl image. She's nice . . . and kind . . . and fun! I think the fame and the lifestyle went to her head at first and she didn't know how to handle it. It all happened so quickly, you see. But it wasn't as bad as it seemed. The media hyped it up.'

'They always do,' says Tash who reads all the celebrity magazines and knows about these things.

'And now she's with Greg . . . I mean Titch . . . she's calmed down a lot.'

'Ahh, Titch!' Everyone's eyes look dreamy – even

Dani's. 'Titch' Mooney: tall, dark, drop-dead gorgeous striker for West Park Wanderers, the darling of women everywhere.

Aka Greg Mooney, Nikki's boyfriend. The press never call him by his real name. He is always referred to as *Titch* because he is so big. It's what's known as being ironic. Like Dad calls me *Trouble* and Nikki *Angel*.

'You were wrong about Alana de Silva being the hottest person on the planet, Tash,' remarks Dani, grinning widely. 'It's Titch, every time. Now I've seen him in the flesh.'

We all start to giggle as we think back to last night.

After the audience had got over the shock of seeing Alana de Silva supporting the FC label on Riverside Academy's catwalk, I had one more surprise in store for them. Another set of people had made their entrance on stage. People who had even more right than we did to wear an FC label.

WPWFC to be precise.

West Park Wanderers Football Club.

Persuaded by their captain, Titch Mooney, the whole squad had given up their Friday night to come along to our school and help us raise money.

Everyone screamed as they appeared on the catwalk. They'd ditched their tracksuits, you see. Greg and I had sourced something else for them to wear instead.

Eco-friendly, sustainable, organic bamboo and hemp UNDERPANTS.

That's all.

'Did you see my mum's face?' squawks Lissa, and I shriek, 'Did you see my dad's?' and then we all start gabbling at once.

'What about Mrs Shepherd?'

'I thought she was going to faint on the spot!'

'I thought she was going to have a fit!'

'But then the whole audience got to their feet . . .'

'Even my dad!' I say, still in shock.

'And everyone was clapping and cheering . . .'

'And whistling . . .'

'And stamping their feet . . .'

'So she got up and joined in too!' splutters Tash and we all howl with laughter and everyone in the cafe is staring at us, but I don't care.

'It was brilliant!' says Lissa.

'Awesome!' says Dani.

'What a way to end an amazing night!' says Tash.

'Aaahhh!' Four happy people give a deep sigh of satisfaction and all goes quiet.

Then Lissa says, 'It was all down to you, Ali.'

'Not just me,' I protest. 'You and Austen, Nikki and Greg . . .'

'No, it was you,' she insists, generously. 'You and your sister. You were the masterminds behind it all.'

'It's true,' says Tash. 'Your dad should be very proud of his Grimes Girls.' And I try to look modest but I can't help grinning from ear to ear. Because he is.

I jump to my feet. 'I'm just proud to be one of the Gang of Four! Come here, you lot!' I open my arms wide to encircle my lovely friends, and squeeze them tight.

And then, together, we all make a solemn promise to each other.

'NO MORE SECRETS!'

Things I will always remember about last night

- Riverside Academy's Great Hall transformed into the most glittering, star-studded fashion event of the year.
- Austen, tie-dyeing, surrounded by a host of admiring girls, looking not in the least bit geeky.
- Tash's face when Alana de Silva came on the stage.
- Mrs Shepherd's face when WPWFC came on the stage.
- Lissa and Tash, seriously glam in their mums' dresses.
- Tomboy Dani, tough, stylish, sexy.
- Miss Webb, pretty and pink and not a bit like a teacher, surrounded by men in their underpants.
- My dad, turning round to Mrs Hamilton

and saying, 'Alana de Silva. That's my girl.'

- Mrs Hamilton looking impressed.
- Nikki, on stage at the end, saying, 'My little sister, Alice Grimes, did all this. She's way cooler than me.'
- Me, hugging my sister, and everyone cheering and clapping us and stamping their feet.
- The Barbies gazing up at me, green with envy.
- And, best of all, the Gang of Four dancing together on the stage, Alana and Titch dancing with us, and the whole audience up on their feet and rocking.

No More Secrets

Alice's secret is out and the friends have promised
NO MORE SECRETS!
But can they keep to it? Could Tash, Lissa
or Dani be hiding something too?

Don't miss the next book in the
Secrets Club series coming soon.

Are YOU in the Secrets Club? Join up at
www.secretsclubbooks.com

Bright and shiny and sizzling with fun stuff . . .

puffin.co.uk

WEB FUN

UNIQUE and exclusive digital content!
Podcasts, photos, Q&A, Day in the Life of, interviews
and much more, from Eoin Colfer, Cathy Cassidy,
Allan Ahlberg and Meg Rosoff to Lynley Dodd!

WEB NEWS

The **Puffin Blog** is packed with posts and photos from
Puffin HQ and special guest bloggers. You can also sign up
to our monthly newsletter **Puffin Beak Speak**

WEB CHAT

Discover something new EVERY month –
books, competitions and treats galore

WEBBED FEET

(Puffins have funny little feet and
brightly coloured beaks)

Point your mouse our way today!

It all started with a Scarecrow.

Puffin is seventy years old.
Sounds ancient, doesn't it? But Puffin has never been
so lively. We're always on the lookout for the next big
idea, which is how it began all those years ago.

Penguin Books was a big idea from the mind of
a man called Allen Lane, who in 1935 invented
the quality paperback and changed the world.
**And from great Penguins, great Puffins grew,
changing the face of children's books forever.**

The first four Puffin Picture Books were hatched in 1940 and the
first Puffin story book featured a man with broomstick arms called
Worzel Gummidge. In 1967 Kaye Webb, Puffin Editor, started the
Puffin Club, promising to **'make children into readers'**.
She kept that promise and over 200,000 children became
devoted Puffineers through their quarterly instalments of
Puffin Post, which is now back for a new generation.

Many years from now, we hope you'll look back and
remember Puffin with a smile. **No matter what your age
or what you're into, there's a Puffin for everyone.**
The possibilities are endless, but one thing is for sure:
whether it's a picture book or a paperback, a sticker book
or a hardback, **if it's got that little Puffin
on it – it's bound to be good.**